D0277825

WHATEVER HAPPENED TO RACHEL?

Dedicated to My Mum with love.

First published in 2001 by The Healing Place
Ettrick Bank, Ettrickbridge, Selkirk TD7 5JL
Scotland
All Rights Reserved

A catalogue record for this book is available from
The British Library.

ISBN 0-9538691-1-3

Printed for The Healing Place by
Meigle Printers Ltd.
Tweedbank Industrial Estate
Galashiels

PROLOGUE

In the executive lounge at Los Angeles airport sat a tanned, good looking man in his middle to late fifties. He looked relaxed and at ease. He was in deep conversation with an elderly lady traveller. She was apparently charmed by his attention and she had insisted that he be allowed to accompany her into this restricted area for a drink, prior to flying. The airport official at the desk had tried to explain that only travellers, holding first class or business class tickets, were allowed entry. But, seeing that the lady traveller was about to cause a scene, he relented, noting that the gentleman in question did, at least, look respectable.

The flight to London was delayed and the facilities of the executive lounge suited Terry Harrison admirably. He had always felt that he was at home in such surroundings and it was only through unfortunate circumstances and incredible runs of bad luck, that he had never aspired to the life of the rich and famous.

A copy of The Times lay on the table in front of him and, as he reached for his glass of malt whisky, his eye fell on an obituary notice. There was a photograph of a man he used to know many years ago. He picked up the newspaper and stared at it.......

'Thomas Oldfield, beloved husband of the late Harriet Oldfield a wealthy businessman and benefactor – died peacefully in his sleep, after a short illness, on April 22nd. Thomas Oldfield is survived by his only daughter, Rachel.'

ONE

The woman sat by the table, her weight heavy on the chair. She lent forward, her elbows balanced either side of a half eaten bowl of cereal, forehead resting on her hands. A cooling mug of coffee, half consumed, had been pushed aside to make room for the morning paper.

This was a pleasant room, small with a low ceiling. The brightness of the window and the view beyond lightened the kitchen and gave it a feeling of space. A glass door, leading to a paved area, stood open. The freshness of the summer morning filled the room. Bright geraniums, in a cluster of terra cotta pots, crowded the patio and there was a scent of moist earth, of leaves and grass and honeysuckle.

The silence of the room was interrupted by the delicate sound of silvery wind chimes which hung close to the open doorway. In the distance, from the fields beyond, there was the plaintive sound of sheep.

The woman did not move. She would not have heard these sounds or smelt the honeysuckle or noticed the vibrancy of the geraniums. She was not here in this room. She had slipped away to some faraway place – somewhere she did not want to be. She was troubled by some memory best forgotten. She was so still – quite motionless, like some sculpture, as if indeed she had been turned to stone. She looked transfixed – trance like.

She seemed broken and carried an air of unspeakable sadness and utter desolation.

She was about forty years old. Her long hair was a lightish brown colour and was tied back by a brightly coloured scarf, giving her a slightly ethnic look.

She had beautiful skin and an olive complexion and the hands, held to her forehead, had long, sensuous fingers and neat, unpolished nails. She wore a simple print dress, open necked with short sleeves and a long flowing skirt. Her legs and arms were bronzed with the sun and her feet were bare. She was slim and of medium height.

Suddenly, the mood of the sunlit room changed! The chair was forced back with the screech of wood on the tiled floor. The woman was on her feet and as she grabbed the blue and white mug half filled with coffee and hurled it across the room, she shouted, "Damn him – Damn him – Damn him!" Her other hand swept across the table sending the cereal bowl and its contents and a jug of milk in the opposite direction.

At the same time a large grey cat, who had been sitting silently and patiently underneath the table hoping for a saucer of milk, hurled its terrified body through the patio door and fled into the distance like the proverbial 'bat out of Hell'.

It was apparent that this change of mood and sudden release of anger had helped the woman. She snatched up the paper – the cause of this outburst and headed, after the cat, into the garden with a purposeful stride.

She marched angrily across the patio, down the stone steps and over the lawn to the far end of the beautifully landscaped garden.

In the far corner she sat down on a wooden bench tucked away under a large swaying willow tree, its fronds almost brushing the ground in places. This was a favourite place – a place where she had often found comfort and peace – a safe haven – somewhere she could think clearly and find inner stillness.

She sat there, eyes closed, gathering herself, allowing her body to return to normal. She took a few long, deep breaths and very slowly she began to relax. It was apparent that she had done this many times before and had worked on this means of stress relief over and over again. This was a regime that worked for her. It had been learned and practised and used through difficult times and the powerful strategy was producing the desired effect.

She now appeared calm and controlled and at peace. The

offending paper lay beside her on the bench and it too seemed to have changed. It had lost its potency – its aggressiveness – its dangerous, threatening element - a gun with its bullets removed - the bow with no arrow to shoot.

After several minutes, the woman slowly opened her eyes and smiled. She stretched out her long, brown legs and raised her arms upwards to their full length allowing her head to move backwards and her smile went out to the blue sky above.

The grey cat, hidden in the undergrowth, was watching her and it too had begun to relax and recover from its shock. The woman felt ready now to take another look at the offending article in the newspaper which lay, like a defused bomb, by her side. She swallowed and, fighting to remain calm and rational, she lifted the newspaper and read the item several times. She read the script. She examined the words. She read between the lines and she analysed the journalist's intent.

She sat immersed in thought, a faraway look in her deep blue eyes, then she read it all again.

Her attention now moved to the grey and white picture which accompanied the article. A face she vaguely recognised looked back at her. She remembered this person – this young woman. A lifetime ago these had been her eyes. That fair curling hair had been brushed and arranged by her hands. And that dress – oh how she remembered that dress! How she had hated that blue dress! She could still see its pale blue material with its tiny white spots. Its neat white collar and dainty sleeves, its shapeless skirt touching her knees. That dress – he had chosen it and insisted she wear it. All the feelings flooded back. She felt sick and her hands began to shake.

Hurriedly she pushed the paper away as if it was infected – a threat to her life. She moved along the bench and once more closed her eyes, slowed her breathing and went within.

This time, when she stretched and smiled again, she got to her feet and, ignoring the paper, she headed back to the house. She disappeared inside and returned moments later and sank into a comfortable chair on the patio, a steaming mug of tea in her hands.

She was still lost in thought as she sipped the tea, both hands wrapped around the mug, enjoying its warmth.

She was obviously still troubled but she was now in control. She had decided that she would deal with whatever it was bit by bit, not rushing, with full awareness. This was a huge challenge but she had a strength which had been built up from the very lowest depths, piece by piece – lesson by lesson – insight by insight – layer upon layer of physical, mental, emotional and spiritual growth. It was a rock solid foundation built from the wreckage, the anguish and desolation and degradation of a complete mental breakdown.

It had taken years – lost years but certainly not wasted years. She had been to Hell and back and had, until that morning, been moving steadily and haltingly forward.

At the bottom of the garden lay the offending newspaper, discarded and abandoned. It was folded open at an inside page.

Half way down the page, in the right hand bottom corner, was a picture of a young girl aged about twenty. She had a look of simple beauty – a naivety – an unworldliness. Her hair was fair and softly curled around her gentle face and onto her shoulders. She was slim and the dress she wore was simple, almost prim, buttoned high to the neck with a small, white, lace collar. The hem line of the dress touched her knee. She looked demure in an almost old fashioned sort of way. The tops of her arms were hidden under short neat sleeves trimmed with lace to match the collar. The headline for the article which accompanied the picture read – WHATEVER HAPPENED TO RACHEL.......?

It appeared from the article that Rachel, the young girl in the photograph, was being searched for by her estranged husband. They had, apparently, parted several years ago. It was a tragic story.

Rachel and Terry had fallen desperately in love when Rachel was only eighteen and still at school, much to the disapproval of her wealthy father. They ran off and married and were, according to the newspaper, blissfully happy even though relations remained strained between Rachel and her father. Rachel chose to give up plans for a University education, hoping to devote her life to being a wife and subsequently, a mother.

After three years she did indeed, to their great joy, become pregnant. All was well until, after an accident in the home, Rachel miscarried a baby boy in the sixth month of pregnancy. Rachel and Terry were both devastated by their loss. Rachel became depressed and withdrawn. She shut herself away and gave up on life for a while.

About eighteen months later, when she seemed to be recovering from her depression, her husband went away for a few days. He was a teacher and he was leading a field trip with a group of students. When he returned he found his beautiful young wife in high spirits. Imagine his surprise when he found a baby boy sleeping peacefully in a pram in the corner of the sitting room. When he asked Rachel who's baby she was minding, she had looked surprised and answered "He's ours of course, Silly!"

When Terry turned on the news the awful truth became apparent. The search was still continuing for the missing infant taken, in his pram from outside the supermarket in the High Street, two days previously.

Terry had had no choice but to inform the authorities immediately. He also called in the family doctor for Rachel's protection.

Rachel was charged with the abduction of the child but was unfit to stand trial having to be sectioned under the Mental Health Act and admitted to a psychiatric hospital. Rachel refused to have Terry anywhere near her and he did not see her for nearly two years.

Rachel's father came back into Rachel's life at this time and paid for her treatment and care to be carried out in the finest private clinic. He gave strict instructions via the medical staff that his son-in-law was not, on any account, to be allowed to visit.

Terry was distraught, desperate to support and care for his sick young wife. He rang the clinic, sent flowers and tender loving messages which never, he believed, reached her. He carried on with his job, looked after the home and waited for the day when his beautiful young wife would return to him, her mental health restored.

Rachel, at this time, he said, became completely dominated by her powerful father and the doctors he had found for her. They all contrived to turn her against him. There was nothing he could do. The legal system was powerless to intervene.

When eventually he was allowed to see his wife, it was a shock. She had changed so much. She had put on an immense amount of weight probably due to the drugs she had been taking. She seemed to have lost her youthful freshness. She had aged about twenty years. Her eyes were dull and lifeless and her movements sluggish. In fact he hardly recognised her. Her voice was low and monotonous and she said very little. When he went to hug her she stiffened and turned away. A male psychiatric nurse watched with a protective eye. They were like strangers.

Rachel had at last come to terms with what she had done and recognised that the baby she had taken belonged to someone else. She had faced again the realisation that their baby had died. However she was still, he could see, far from well. The visit seemed to have little affect on Rachel though it was a devastatingly disappointing reunion for Terry.

He continued to visit regularly over the next twelve months and slowly, very slowly they began to talk, and very occasionally he saw a glimpse of the girl he had fallen in love with and married. Eventually Rachel did return home to Terry but after a few years she had had another breakdown. Their marriage had disintegrated and they lost touch with one another.

TWO

Mary Parker, nowadays, did nothing in a hurry. The impetuosity of her youth had disappeared long ago. She had learned strategies and had been programmed over the years by therapists, psychologists and counsellors. Now she had developed her own coping skills and they were never rushed. Events and incidents no longer propelled her into immediate action. She stood back from situations, allowing the heat and intensity to wane, before she did anything. She found this much less stressful and it seemed to work for her. Often by the time she was ready to deal with a situation it had already resolved itself.

This, she realised, was perhaps her biggest test so far. She doubted very much that this hurdle would just go away but she trusted her proven system and stepped back from the problem. She did not forget it but instead of wrestling with it constantly, she took it out and looked at it, at times of her choosing, then put it back again, as if she lifted a book from the bookshelf, read it for a while, then returned it to its place until another time. She would then perhaps paint or sketch, take a walk in the fields, play the piano or work in the garden for a while.

Mary Parker had lived in this house for three years now. It was rented and she liked the feeling of impermanence this gave her. It was hers but not her responsibility. If she had to move on suddenly she could just pack up and go.

She had come to love this house and its garden and the open countryside beyond was a great joy to her. She had felt safe here and this was so important to her.

The house was in a small country town. The front was on to a street but strangely had no windows at all on this frontal aspect. It was as if it had been built back to front. From the roadway it looked dull and unattractive and unremarkable, hardly noticeable. Mary had chosen the house mainly because of these features. No one could look through her windows. After years of hospitalisation this privacy was like running water to a man who had spent years in the desert.

The neighbouring properties were separated from the side windows by trees and high hedges and the back of the house overlooked the garden and the open countryside beyond. It was an ideal home for someone who wanted to retreat from the outside world.

Mary had made no friends since moving here and the local people had decided that she was rather odd. She was on nodding terms with a number of people and would pass the time of day with neighbours, shopkeepers etc. but they knew nothing at all about her. She never had any visitors. She did go to the church quite regularly and was on the flower rota. She usually attended the early morning services and slipped in and out quietly, not stopping to chat.

Her immediate neighbours had tried to be friendly when she first moved in but she had not encouraged them and they just waved and nodded when they saw one another. She knew nothing about them and they knew nothing about her and that was how she hoped it would remain.

She had got to know the children next door, Tom and his sister, Cathy. They had come round on numerous occasions to collect balls of various sizes and colours which had crossed the hedge into her garden. Children were different. They were bound up in their own lives and unconcerned about who she was or where she had come from.

Cathy was a bright, confident, attractive seven year old when Mary first met her. Her blonde bouncing hair and deep blue eyes reminded Mary of the child she had once been. Cathy's energy and enthusiasm and absolute belief in herself and her capabilities were again like those of that long forgotten adolescent. What had become of that spirited being? What or who had damaged that child or young person? She knew the answers now to both these questions.

Tom, on the other hand, was small for his five years, less secure in himself. He was a beautiful little boy. He had dark brown hair and even darker eyes. He was slower in every way than his sister. He was growing up in her shadow. He was sensitive and gentle and had an open loving heart. He was filled with kindness and it still surprised him when he found this absent in other people.

Mary watched the development of both children with a knowing eye. She had that perception and understanding only attained by people who, like she, had spent years in and out of psychotherapy. People who, in order to reach some degree of sanity and order in their broken lives, had had to analyse, bit by bit, the things in their past which had almost destroyed their mental stability. She, more than most, had begun to work out what had happened to the carefree little child she had once been.

One day, about six months after she had moved in, Mary was sitting at the bottom of the garden, contentedly gazing into the distance – beyond the fence, across the meadow, past the stream and into the far reaches of the distant hills. In her mind she was sitting on some high ledge on the far away hillside. She could feel the fresh mountain air in her hair. She could smell the blue hare-bells and the bracken. She could hear the wind in her ears and the sound of a skylark. She was enveloped in the peacefulness of her imagined surroundings.

She was brought back to reality by the sounds of raised voices and a child's high pitched angry scream from the garden next door — a girl's voice wailing to her mother in distress. The mother's voice raised in anger as she scolded her son for some misdemeanor. Mary cringed as she heard the words being directed like arrows at the young boy, Tom, from next door.

"Get out of my sight, you naughty boy. You are a waste of space. You make a mess of everything. Go on. Get out!"

Mary felt each word for the boy. She knew from long experience the lasting damage such words could inflict if heard often enough.

A moment later she saw Tom. He was in the field and he was running as fast as his legs could carry him. Every movement showed his anger, his hurt, his frustration. He had already found his own strategy – his means of coping.

Mary knew all about exercises for anger release. Had she not tried them all? The pillows she had pounded – the screams she had screamed, her voice damaged for days – her throat raw. It all came back to her as she watched Tom run and run. She could make out his small exhausted figure now prostrate on the bank at the far edge of the meadow. Was he, she wondered, pounding the ground or was he perhaps sobbing his heart out to the distant hills?

Mary closed her eyes. She felt an intruder. This was a private time for Tom. This was a personal thing, not done for effect – not meant to be viewed. In a little while he might want a friend – someone to talk to – but not yet.

Mary went back to her place on the high hillside and in her mind Tom was beside her – sitting quietly – her arm around his small shoulders.

When next Mary opened her eyes and scanned the meadow she could not, at first, see Tom. He was almost hidden as he sat in a clump of high waving grass, tall golden buttercups and purple tipped clover. She could just make out the dark head as he sat arms clutched round his legs, chin resting on his knees.

Now, she thought, this might be the right time. She went back to the house and picked up her sketch pad and a bottle of apple juice – a favourite of Tom's – and made her way into the meadow.

She did not go directly towards Tom. She, of all people, would never push her way into someone else's space. She walked in a straight line towards the far end of the meadow – her course several metres away from Tom's hiding place.

She looked straight ahead as she drew level with the small boy. As she moved beyond him a small voice called out, "Hi, Mary. Where are you going?"

"Oh, hello, Tom." Mary sounded surprised. "I didn't see you there. I'm going nowhere in particular. How about you?"

"That's where I was thinking of going. Can I come with you?" He asked as he walked tentatively towards her, his eyes bright and wet with tears.

"Yes, why not. Let's go nowhere together. I believe it's a very interesting place!" She held out her hand to the small boy. "Will you carry the bottle for me?"

The two walked companionably towards the bank of the small stream and sat down side by side.

"Have a drink if you like." Mary said and she reached into the deep pockets of her flowing skirt and pulled out two chocolate bars.

Tom looked at her adoringly as only a child can and said a polite thank you.

She would have loved to hug him but this was not how they were with one another. She did not treat him as a small boy and he did not look upon her as an adult figure. This was the beauty of their growing relationship. They were friends, sensitive to each other's needs. They seemed to understand one another and they felt comfortable together.

Mary lifted her sketch pad and drew out pencils from her pocket.

"Do you want to draw, Tom?" she asked.

"No" he said "I can't. I'm useless. I'm no good at anything." His voice was sad and sort of resigned. He believed what he'd been told. "Mummy says I'm a waste of space!" He sighed.

"Does she?" Mary asked.

"She was mad at me when she said it. I'd pulled Cathy's hair when she was horrid to me about my painting. Then I accidentally knocked over my dirty painting water all over her homework. I didn't mean to do that but she told Mummy I'd done it on purpose and she believed her. And I didn't. I really didn't! Mummy shouted at me and told me to get out of her sight. Cathy said my painting was a mess and a baby could do better. And she's right. I can't do anything."

Mary chose her words with care, "I think you paint very well for your age, Tom. I don't think you are a waste of space. I enjoy when you spend time with me." His shoulders raised and he turned towards her, listening. "You know, Tom." Mary went on. "It's not what other people think about us that is important – it is what we think about ourselves that really matters!"

Tom did not say anything for a bit. It was clear that he was thinking about what she had said. Eventually he said, "You mean that just because Cathy says my painting is rubbish, I don't have to believe her?"

"Yes." Mary said. "If you like your painting that's what counts. Not everyone likes the same things, do they? We like apple juice but some people hate it. I like black coffee and you like it with lots of milk. Do you see what I mean?"

"Right" he said "I like banana sandwiches and Cathy can't stand them. She likes scrambled eggs and I like them boiled. Yes, I think I see. I think I will do some drawing now."

Mary handed the boy a piece of paper from her sketch pad and some card to lean on and a sharply pointed pencil.

The two sat quietly together fully occupied in what they were doing. Neither spoke for some time. Eventually the boy laid down his paper and pencil and moved behind Mary to see what she was drawing. On the paper was an exquisite drawing of a patch of dandelions. Some were in full flower, others were covered in their magical circle of seeds. The leaves were spiked in their characteristic shapes. They came alive on the paper.

"That's lovely, Mary" Tom said.

"Thank you, Tom" Mary smiled. "I like it too. Let me see what you've been doing."

Tom hesitated, then reluctantly and with an apprehensive look at Mary, he held out his drawing.

"That's wonderful, Tom" Mary said. "I can see your house and mine next door. Is that me in the garden?"

"Yes," Tom beamed and it was as if the sun had come out. "Do you really like it?"

She nodded and smiled.

"Well I want you to keep it. It's a present."

"Oh thank you, Tom. But don't you want to show it to Mummy first?"

"No" he said. "She won't like it and Cathy will laugh at it." His small face clouded over and the sunshine of a moment ago had disappeared. Mary wished she had kept her last remark to herself.

"But do you like it, Tom? That's the most important thing, remember!"

Tom looked hard at his picture. Then he nodded "Yes, I do like it. This is a very good picture!"

They looked at each other and laughed.

There was a call from the other side of the field. Tom's mother was waving and calling his name. Tom got up, pressed the picture into Mary's hand and was on his way home at full speed.

She smiled after him and tucked the picture into her sketch pad.

THREE

Mary had kept the newspaper and referred back to it several times over the days that followed. She kept a close eye on the daily paper to see if there were any follow up articles. She felt sure there was more to come.

About five days later her fears were proved right. A second article relating to the missing Rachel appeared on page five of the newspaper.

Mary was less shocked but similarly affected by the newsprint. She read the article thoroughly then left the paper on the kitchen table and went outside. It was as if she needed to distance herself from something offensive – breathe some fresh air and look at something beautiful.

The article was shorter than the previous one but it too had an accompanying picture. The girl in this photograph was a schoolgirl and again, blonde and pretty. She looked about fourteen or fifteen years old.

This was, it appeared, Marianne Phillips, the young daughter of Mr. and Mrs. Earnest Phillips, who had, according to the newspaper, run off with her forty one year old teacher, ten years before. She had, it transpired, been found fairly quickly by the police and returned safely to her anxious parents. The teacher in question had been prosecuted and given a custodial sentence.

The teacher involved was a certain Mr. Terry Harrison – the previously mentioned loving husband of the missing Rachel! The man who was so eager to locate his ex-wife.

Perhaps, the article concluded, the public should be less ready to help reunite these former lovers. The missing Rachel might well have good reason for wanting not to be found!

Mary puzzled over these newspaper articles. What, she wondered, was going on? She was certain that Terry had been the instigator of the first article. What was he up to? With a chilling certainty, she knew the answer!

The second article was certainly not of Terry's choosing. Was this, she wondered, the work of some eager investigative journalist or had someone else contacted the newspaper with this latest revelation? And where, she asked herself, would it go next.....?

She felt apprehensive. She was involved but somehow she felt distanced from it. Perhaps it would all blow over – a story with no conclusion. It was as if a stick had stirred up the mud at the bottom of a pond and slowly, if left undisturbed, the dirt would gradually settle, sink to the bottom again and the water would become clear and untroubled once more. How she hoped that this might be so but she had a deep foreboding that this would not be the case.

Mary knew that she had changed, but not Terry. He would be like a dog with a bone – gnawing and wrestling with it. Seeking out Rachel would be the complete focus of all his attention. He would not let go!

As Mary brushed her teeth that evening she looked at herself closely in the mirror. She could look herself in the eye now, and yes, she liked the person reflected there. This had taken years and years of work and she was still working at it. Every day she had self esteem exercises to do – every day she was alert to any negative thoughts she might have. She wrote in her journal each day. Her journals were lined up – shelf after shelf of inner work and soul searching – personal analysis, leading to personal growth and she believed, freedom. This work had been her salvation.

Mary Parker was no lover of the media. The person she had once been had featured in the headlines on more than one occasion. She knew, more than most, how awful it could be to have the media on your trail and how horrific and devastating it could be.

She hoped that her new identity would remain unknown, unrecognised and of no interest to anyone.

She looked again at the person looking out of the mirror. Would anyone see in this face the image of that young woman in last week's newspaper? Her hair was now a reddish brown colour. It was long and was usually worn straight back from her face in a knot at the back of her head. Her eyes of course were still blue but, whenever she went out, she hid them behind tinted glasses. She was of course older – almost twenty years older. Where had these years gone? Her complexion was still good and the few lines around her eyes and mouth gave her a look of maturity rather than aging.

She smiled to herself and let her eyes smile back to her. Her teeth were white and even. This was a warm smile and she enjoyed the giving and receiving of it.

Mary Parker moved in a graceful relaxed manner – she almost seemed to glide. Each part of her body was in complete harmony. There was a fascinating laziness in her movements. It was as if her physical body had attuned to the changes in her mental and emotional attitude. Over the years she had learned and practiced tai chi and yoga and the way she moved gave evidence of these arts.

She had turned a small bedroom into a sort of sanctuary – a quiet place. It was here that she did her daily meditation, her various exercises for body, mind and spirit. On the walls were bookshelves, prints and photographs of beautiful landscapes, sunsets and wide ocean views. A small table, covered with a deep purple cloth, held a few exquisite pieces of quartz crystal, an assortment of candles and a carved Buddha type figure.

There was a music centre in one corner and the room was often filled with wonderful music – sometimes haunting, sometimes uplifting and sometimes deeply spiritual.

There were three chairs to suit any mood. One was deep and soft – the kind which seems to hug you as you sink into its soft cushions. There was a low chair with no arms and a higher straight backed wooden chair and in the corner, close to the floor, was a small meditation stool, the kind seen in Buddhist temples.

The books on the shelves were a very mixed collection – mostly new-age type material, covering a vast range of subjects from complementary medicines to books on various religions, to books on art and literature.

This was a place where a person could not only unwind and find peace but it was also a place where one could discover new directions and broaden one's knowledge and outlook on life.

The shelves in this room did not house the dozens of journals. These books would not have sat comfortably in this place of tranquility. The emotional trauma and turmoil, the extremes of emotion they contained, surrounded them in an unpleasant energy. The associations connected with them were hard for the writer of them to acknowledge. She hated them and what they stood for but she could not, as yet, part with them.

It was unlikely that she would ever read them again and they were certainly not for sharing. Much of them would probably be illegible – the writing twisted and disrupted by the depth of the emotions being expressed and released. Some parts were in a childlike hand as the emotions of a young child were recorded – there were accompanying drawings on some pages. There were parts written in the most beautiful moving prose and others where the language was violent and obscene. Some pages were scrawled with one or two words, over and over again, recording times of unutterable, inexpressible misery and self loathing.

As an illustration of a mind in the depths and complexities of severe mental illness and the slow, hesitant steps leading out of the abyss, these journals were a window to it all.

Mary needed these journals as a reminder of where she had been and of just how far she had travelled. She was not yet ready to destroy them. One day she knew she would have progressed that far, but not yet.

These journals were bunched together on a high shelf in a room she hardly ever used. She knew they were there, but she did not have to look at them.

Her daily journals now were a source of inspiration and insight and these journals of recent years were bound in bright attractive covers and were proudly stacked in the bookcase near the patio doors. Sometimes she wrote poetry or beautifully written meditative journeys. She would, she thought, write a book one day.

Mary was also a talented artist. Her art work, like her writing, had begun as part of her therapy. Her pictures were no longer the lost and angry works of earlier years – frightening, tormented canvases of darkness or vibrant, lurid colours tearing across the scenes in frantic, terrorised outbursts. Nowadays she worked gently and lovingly and could captivate the unseen beauty in many of her subjects.

She enjoyed her talents but did not share them. She had no one to share them with, only little Tom, she did share with him. He had somehow manoeuvred his way into her life and though she did not know it yet, into her heart.

Tom, with the innocence of a small child, had been oblivious to the barriers all around Mary. He did not see them. He was not put off by her unapproachable manner and he ignored her quiet ways. He would just appear and sit quietly beside her as she painted. He would arrive beside her and carry her weeds to the wheelbarrow or sit and watch her as she tied up the herbaceous plants. He did not speak or chatter or ask endless questions like most little children, he just let his gentle presence mingle with hers.

One day a few months after Mary had moved into her house, she was lost in her music, sitting at her piano, just playing for the love of it, when she became aware that the small boy from next door had crept indoors from the garden and was sitting, very quietly, watching her, his fingers moving in time to the music, a look of contentment on his face.

That was the day they became friends. She smiled at the small figure and said, "Hello, Tom. I didn't hear you come in. Would you like a drink?"

Tom's mother had told Mary that she must send him home if he became a nuisance but she never found him in her way and, when he was missing from home, the family next door always knew where he would be.

Cathy sometimes came with Tom but it all seemed rather dull to her and she soon became bored and went home, much to their relief.

On the day the newspaper brought disharmony into Mary's quiet orderliness she sat deep in thought by the fish pond in the afternoon sunshine. She had gone off on a mental journey and was far away. She was unable that day to maintain her vision – troubled thoughts – disturbing memories kept intruding and she sighed. Just then a small boy slipped down beside her without saying a word and a small, suntanned hand rested very gently on her knee. The two sat like that for a while and Mary did not feel quite so alone.

FOUR

Mary had never been particularly religious. The family had always attended their local church regularly and her father had enjoyed being the church's local benefactor. Funds for a new roof or new bells were always forthcoming. If a place in heaven could be bought then her father had bought and paid for the very best accommodation.

In her childhood years Mary had not needed a god particularly. She had enjoyed the rituals of the church services and festivals. She enjoyed dressing up in 'Sunday best' clothes and she loved the music and she sang in the choir with enthusiasm when she was old enough.

During her illness she had hated God as she had hated everyone and everything, especially herself. It was only in recent years that she had found comfort again in the church, its sacraments and its peaceful orderliness. She loved the quietness and the reverence found in sacred buildings. She felt safe and somehow comforted within a church. This too was the kind of place where it was all right to be on ones own – in fact she really believed it was preferable to be alone – alone with God.

She had no hard and fast rules about who or what God was. She did not feel particularly attached to any one denomination. She was familiar with the ceremony of the Christian Church but was of the opinion that there were many different ways to God and she felt she would feel the same be it in a monastery, a temple or a synagogue.

She rejected the idea that there was only one true way in which to worship and, in her heart, believed in complete religious and spiritual freedom.

When she had first come to her home in this community she had erected huge protective barriers around herself. She did not want to let anyone or anything near her. Her wounds were healing but were still very raw and painful. She was not yet ready to put her toe into the water. She needed time to adjust to this new environment as well as to her new identity. She wanted to remain invisible – see but not be seen.

That very first week she had slipped inside the small church opposite when a sudden downpour caught her by surprise as she hesitantly and self consciously walked in the graveyard. She was startled and amazed by the emotions which took hold of her as she sank quietly and reverently into a dark pew at the rear of the church.

There was no one in the church and she felt safe and comfortable. Mary had grown used to her own company and had begun to feel at ease with herself but here she felt that she was not alone. It was as if strong, invisible arms held her – a presence was there believing in her, loving her and best of all supporting her. She closed her eyes and relished this new experience. This was no long forgotten sensation. This was a feeling she had never felt before. She wondered if this might be the way a new born infant feels as he is cradled in the arms of a new parent.

Mary opened her eyes after a while, loath to let go of this comforting embrace.

This was a beautiful place – the dark oak of the pews and the arched ceiling seemed to shine. The cushions on the long narrow pews and the kneeling stools were faded but still held a little of their former glory of deep red and gold. The pulpit, wonderfully carved in oak, stood tall and commanding in the left hand frontage of the church. The choir stalls lay silent – chairs standing to attention in neat rows. The font was carved in grey stone with the hollowed top awaiting its blessed water on baptismal Sundays. The communion table was strong and solid and held the silver candlesticks and a heavy silver cross. Piles of red backed bibles, prayer books and hymnals stood on a table by the door with an offering box and a leather bound visitors' book.

Mary could smell the wood, the candle wax and the flowers. A huge vase of white daisies and silvery foliage filled an area opposite the pulpit and in front of the organ. It was all just perfect. She did not want a single thing to change. Apart from the flowers it was probably much as it had always been for hundreds of years.

This consistency, this feeling of permanence was very reassuring to Mary who had not felt like this about anything for a very long time.

How fortunate that the church had been unlocked that afternoon. This must have been an oversight – an exceedingly lucky coincidence.

Since that first time in the church Mary had felt a deep connection with this place. She looked forward to the services there and could enter and exit quietly without being noticed. Eventually she was approached by the vicar and agreed to become part of the flower team. She was then allowed a key to the church and her times, alone in the church, arranging her flowers, were some of her happiest moments in that first year.

FIVE

Very gradually, in the quiet safety of her new environment, Mary was able to relax a little and begin to trust the things which surrounded her. She related to and was comfortable with the garden, the flowers, the soil and the trees. She loved the distant landscape of meadows, stream and hillsides. They gave her a much needed feeling of constancy and dependability. She could trust that they, unlike people, would not let her down. They would change with the seasons but their essence would always be the same.

She was comfortable with the birds and any wildlife which came close to her and she was able to relate to them.

Mary was not yet ready to trust people though the childish innocence of the smile of the boy next door and her growing fondness for him, was a beginning.

One day, about a year after moving into this house, Mary noticed her small neighbour perched on a rock beside her garden pond. His body was hunched and he was gazing into the water, his bright blue anorak pulled tightly round his body. A red and navy rucksack was beside him on the ground. He looked the picture of desolation and misery.

Mary was surprised to find herself moved by this pathetic little figure. Her heart seemed to melt and she experienced a feeling, long since suppressed, fill her being. She empathised with this little boy. She had so often felt the way he was feeling at this moment. It did not make any difference what the reasons were behind this mood or the fleetingness of their nature – the moments of despair and anguish were the same – the intensity of the emotions were the same.

She moved quietly across the garden not sure whether or not to intrude. Tom lifted his head as she approached and Mary gasped inwardly as the look in his dark eyes felt like a blow in her solar plexus. Instinctively her hand moved to this area of her body as she said in a gentle tone, "Tom, whatever's the matter?"

Her kind tone made him sob and a large tear moved slowly down one cheek. It was as if he carried the burdens of the world on his tiny shoulders.

Mary moved nearer and crouched down to bring her eyes in line with his. She did not touch him or intrude into his space. She spoke to him with her eyes and her heart and not with her mouth.

"Oh, Mary" he eventually said. "I'm just so sad and I don't know what to do." As if in explanation he opened his coat to reveal cuddled inside, close to his chest, a tiny grey bundle of fur. It was a very young kitten. It stirred as he moved and looked up at Mary with the most incredible blue eyes as it made the tiniest plaintive mew. The boy's eyes softened as he looked at the small creature and he touched it with the gentlest of fingers. Mary's heart gave another turn and her eyes filled with tears.

"Someone at school gave it to me." Tom explained. "His father was going to drown it if a home couldn't be found. I brought it home but Mummy says we can't keep it because Cathy is allergic and I've to take it back. But I can't. I just can't. So we're running away." He gestured towards the rucksack. "There's nothing else I can do. I won't let anyone drown her!" As he said this a fierce determined look came into his eyes and he pulled his coat protectively around the kitten.

"Oh, Tom" Mary said. "Let's think about this. How about a hot drink and a biscuit before you go? Shall we go inside for a moment and you can tell me your plans?"

Tom thought for a moment and then, very carefully clutching his left hand to the small bundle inside his coat, he picked up his rucksack with his other hand and followed Mary indoors.

Mary busied herself making hot chocolate for Tom and a coffee for herself. She brought out his favourite biscuits – pink wafers. She only bought them for Tom.

Tom kept his coat on and his rucksack close at hand. It was as if he might have to make a run for it at any moment. He was obviously not about to be persuaded to return home.

"Where do you plan to go?" Mary asked.

"I don't know yet." Tom replied. "I'll probably find a cave or somewhere. We'll be all right. I have some milk for the kitten and crisps and things for me. They're in there." He pointed to the rucksack. "I've got money too – three pounds and eighty seven pence. I took it out of my bank. I thought if I stayed away long enough – just until the kitten is bigger - they won't be able to drown it. Will they, Mary?"

Mary had come to a decision. "Would it help, Tom, if I kept the kitten here for you?" she asked quietly. "She would still be your cat but she could live here with me and you could visit as often as you liked. She'd be safe with me, don't you think?"

"Mary, would you really do that? Would you? You mean she could live here, right next door?" His eyes were bright and sparkling. "That would be perfect. Not quite as good as having her live with me – but the next best thing, and she wouldn't get lonely when I'm at school. Oh thank you, Mary, thank you!" He got down from his chair and, opening his coat, moved towards Mary. Very tenderly he lifted the sleeping bundle of grey fur and held the kitten out to Mary.

The kitten was small enough to sit in the palm of Mary's hand. She stroked its head with one finger. Her eyes met Tom's and they smiled. They were joined in love and compassion for the tiny, defenseless creature who's life they were saving.

Mary was aware that she was making a commitment here – allowing herself to become attached to another living thing. This had not been her intention but somehow it had happened and part of her felt glad.

Mary and Tom prepared a shopping list – things they would need for the kitten, cat litter and a litter tray, a soft bedding basket and some kitten food as well as extra milk. Mary said that they had better let the vet check her out and see what advice he could give on her future requirements and care.

"Well, Tom," Mary said. "I think you had better go next door and let your Mummy know that I am going to share my home with our friend here. Ask if you can come out with me to buy some things we need from the pet shop. We can go straight away if you like."

Tom disappeared and was back again in next to no time with his mother's permission.

How Mary enjoyed that outing. She felt part of the real world again. The shopkeeper did great business that day. The two left the shop laden down with goods. It was impossible to believe that such a tiny scrap could require so much equipment in order to survive.

Mary felt herself becoming childlike as she and Tom focused on their shared delight. They were, she felt, like proud parents looking dotingly on their first born – hearts overflowing with pride and unconditional love.

This kitten was their delight, the absolute centre of their lives. The deep connection between the woman and the small boy was firmly cemented and grew steadily from the appearance of the tiny ball of fur into their lives.

The naming of the kitten was left to Tom. He chose the name Shadow after much deliberation. The vet confirmed that the kitten was female and they were told about the importance of worming, spaying and regular injections. Mary wondered what she had taken on. She felt as if she was putting down roots and taking on responsibilities as well as forming attachments. She liked the way this made her feel but it was exactly what she had promised herself she would never do again. Still, she reassured, herself, it was only a small boy and a cat, not some major emotional entanglement.

These new emotions, the stirrings in her solar plexus and in her heart, knocked her off balance for a time, but she dealt with this and worked through it as she did everything, by journaling her thoughts and feelings, by sitting in the silence and slowly accepting them within her emotional being. This process, having been internalised, allowed Mary to feel comfortable and even happy with the changes in her environment. She delighted in the small furry animal. It's antics made her laugh and its small body as it curled into her neck, purring contentedly, began to ease some of the deep hurts of her past. Tom's constant visits when Shadow was an adorable, fun loving kitten were breaths of fresh air. The house seemed to shake with shrieks and squeals of delight as Tom and Shadow frolicked and played together.

As the months passed and Shadow grew into a strikingly beautiful grey cat and became more independent Tom's visits were less frequent and less boisterous. The household settled down into a quiet homeliness which it had never had before.

The grey cat was a perfect companion. She relaxed beautifully – finding the warmest most comfortable places – patches of sunlight – the centre of armchairs – beside radiators and, in winter, on the rug in front of the log fire. She would sit close to Mary as she painted or read. She would appear silently and join Mary as she meditated. Shadow seemed to enjoy Mary's music and would follow her around the garden as she worked, chasing butterflies, lying in wait for unsuspecting birds or squirrels. She was not a terribly successful hunter much to Mary's relief but she instinctively knew how to lie in wait – motionless, watching and waiting – then, when the time seemed right, she wiggled her rear end and pounced – almost always, a split second too late.

Mary loved to watch her and produced some exquisite pencil drawings of her house mate. That first Christmas after Shadow's arrival, Mary gave Tom a beautiful picture she had painted of Shadow. She had it framed and wrapped and she gave it to Tom when he and Cathy came round on Christmas morning with gifts for her and Shadow. Mary had also done a picture for Cathy – a small pen drawing – a portrait of Cathy which she had done from a quick sketch she had made of the child one afternoon the previous summer. This delighted the little girl, appealing to her innate vanity and self centredness. It was apparent that she viewed the picture not for the skill of the artist but for the beauty of the subject.

Mary smiled at the girl's self assurance and high self value and hoped she would be allowed to keep it and that no one would enter her life and gradually take it all away, piece by piece, layer by layer. This, she knew, was what Terry had done to her over the few years they had been together. This slow, insidious killing of a personality was akin to the slow administration of a deadly poison to the physical body. Both perpetrators were would be murderers, one of the physical body the other of the mental and emotional bodies – of the soul itself.

She had been unaware of what was happening to her – blind to it all until it was too late and she was in no fit mental state to do anything to stop it and had lost the will to fight back.

SIX

Mary closed her eyes and thought about Rachel – the pretty, blue-eyed, blonde, little girl she had been. So like Cathy – confident, energetic, self opinionated and clever – bursting with ideas, competitive – a leader – an adventurer – able to manipulate those around her so that they, for the most part, were unaware it was happening.

Her mother, Harriet Oldfield, had been quiet and, as far as she could remember, easy going – doing all she could to keep life simple and peaceful. Mary now realised that her mother had been completely dominated by her husband and lived totally in his shadow. When Mary looked back she realised that she knew nothing about the woman who had been her mother. She did not know what she had felt about anything – what talents she had, what opinions, what dreams, what fears. Had she been happy in her role of husband and child pleaser? Nobody had ever bothered to ask her. What a sad observation and how sad Mary felt that she could not now ask her mother these questions. Her mother had died soon after Rachel's runaway marriage to Terry. Would things have turned out differently if her mother had lived? Mary thought not – her mother would have been utterly inadequate – unable to help – she would have gone along with what Terry was doing, completely oblivious to what was happening to her daughter – seeing only what it was comfortable to see.

Had her mother, she asked herself, been a bright confident child just as she had been? Had Rachel's father done the same to her mother as Terry had done to her? Had she followed the pattern demonstrated by her parents? She had been down this trail of thought many times and knew it led nowhere.

The way she liked to look at things now was more positive – the hardships, the agonies, even the complete disintegration of her mental capacities had been for a reason. These traumas indeed had led her to become the person she now was. Like a repaired broken bone – her mental strength, as it recovered, was stronger than it had ever been before.

She took heart from this and although she knew that she still had some way to go, she knew with a deep inner knowing and amazing confidence that her mind would never give way again – it might teeter and falter under pressure but it would never ever break again.

Only someone who had suffered a complete mental breakdown could imagine what such a feeling of certainty might mean. Few, she thought, managed such a complete recovery and this freedom from fear of returning to that desert – that no man's land – that barren waste – that place of nothingness, was the most wonderful feeling imaginable.

She was certain that she was indeed free from that fear but she had wrestled with it for many years.

Mary sighed and smiled, the smile of achievement – a long battle overcome – a victory won. And a grey cat rubbed its head into her chin as if to say, well done!

Rachel's father only loved winners. He had no time for losers – also-rans. He was always extremely competitive. He was hard on himself as well as other people. He had made his fortune through untiring effort, dedication and a certain amount of luck. He would never have allowed the word 'luck' to be used – but elements of luck had been there.

Rachel had adored her father as a young child and she rose eagerly to his challenges. She too wanted to be a winner. She soon learned what pleased her father and this goal inspired her in school and on the sports fields. He applauded her successes but always let her know there was further to go. "No use resting on your laurels!" He would say. So it was school to regional finals, then county to national levels. As she grew older she realised that he kept moving the goal posts. Only Olympic gold would have satisfied her father.

She began to tire and fade and perhaps here the first seeds of self doubt, of not being good enough, were sown. This was not done maliciously nor malevolently and certainly not intentionally.

Her father had no time for excuses, the physically or mentally weak, for time wasters. He liked the strong, the determined, life's fighters.

Mary realised that for her father to turn to her so completely when her mental health collapsed must have been an act of complete, unconditional love. It was so out of character for him. It must have torn him apart to see his precious daughter, his only child, in such a state of utter weakness and frailty. She was surprised, when she looked back, that he had not walked away and rejected this failure. But of course he was a fighter and, once he had taken up her cause, he would never have given in. He would have to see it through.

He found for her the best help that money could buy and he listened to the advice of these experts and, all credit to him, he stayed there over the months and years of seemingly little progress. He saw her at the very worst – the apathetic, lifeless piece of flotsam washed up on the beach. Finding himself so helpless and inadequate must have challenged this man of action to the limit. She was aware that her lessons had been his lessons also.

Her father had also had to face feelings of impotence when she fell in love with Terry and decided to give up everything to be with him. Her father had tried – oh, how he had tried to make her see sense. But he was powerless – the more he tried to influence her the more determined she was to defy him. There had been an intense clash of wills and the headstrong fighter he had raised, turned on him, then walked away.

Rachel's father knew that Terry was no good. In his years of business he had become an astute judge of character. He knew that Terry was all too aware of the fortune his only child would one day inherit and he was determined that that day would be a long way off.

He spent hours with various financial advisors and monetary geniuses and experts in the field of financial law working out schemes and trusts to make the moneys less available to his son in law, in the event of his untimely demise.

Rachel and her father were distanced from one another for a time. Strong hurtful words had been said on both sides and a cooling off period was necessary. Rachel vowed that she would never speak to him again and he said something about Hell freezing over first!

When Rachel's mother died suddenly and undramatically – even in death she did not want to cause a fuss, Father and daughter, in their sorrow, forgot their differences and clung to one another in their loss. It surprised them both how much they missed the quiet, unassuming peace maker who had always tried to please everyone. They both had regrets that they had not loved her more.

Terry, of course, was delighted at the reconciliation. He had for some time been urging Rachel to heal the rift with her father.

How obvious it all was in hindsight and with eyes undimmed and unblinkered by the raptures of first love and the rebelliousness of teenage years. What a young fool she had been!

SEVEN

The eighteen year old Rachel had been as vibrant and alive as the sun coming up. She was full of energy, fun and enthusiasm. She lived life, every moment of it, with delight and eager anticipation. Then along came Terry Harrison, a new young Geography teacher, slim, dark and extremely good looking.

Within days Terry had heard about the school's wealthy benefactor – Thomas Oldfield – father of a senior pupil called Rachel. His antenna quivered and when his eyes fell on the blonde, very beautiful heiress, his wit and charm went into action. Rachel did not stand a chance. She was baited and hooked at first cast.

Terry said all the things she wanted to hear. He told her how beautiful she was, how talented and, of course, how much he loved her. It all began in secret because she was still a pupil and he a teacher. This enforced secrecy gave it all a piquancy, a heightened excitement and a touch of adventure, adding fire to the already smouldering emotions in the young girl.

As soon as Rachel left school Terry moved up a gear – flowers and other romantic gifts were delivered to Rachel – little cards with loving messages slipped into her bag when she wasn't looking or tucked under the windscreen wipers of her bright red sports car.

Rachel felt that all her dreams had come true. She was the envy of all her friends.

Terry courted her and told her she was wonderful and that she could do anything she put her mind to. He built up her confidence and self esteem.

She was on top of the world.

Once Terry had caught his fish and the wedding band was on Rachel's finger, very slowly and very cleverly he began to change.

He was still loving and attentive on the surface – still an adoring and model husband to his young bride. The words he said to her, still wrapped in honey, just changed a little – carried hidden messages, undercurrents of doubt – hints that perhaps he should help her – she might not be able to manage on her own. He loved looking after her...... He would always be there if she found she could not cope.

He convinced her that she would not be able to continue her studies and run a home. He undermined her confidence – little hints about the way she did her hair – the clothes she wore. He corrected her in public if she mispronounced a word and questioned her opinions. Gradually she stopped speaking when in company – merely smiled and agreed with her husband. She stopped seeing her friends and settled into her role as wife and homemaker.

She was an excellent cook but somehow Terry always managed to find some fault. He would not criticize the meal, merely make some helpful suggestion, said very lovingly, only to help her. Gradually, as the months passed, Rachel began to feel more and more inadequate, more and more a failure.

Rachel could not believe that this wonderful man had chosen her with all of her shortcomings and she became more uncertain and less secure.

The great joy which Rachel felt when she knew that she was pregnant could not be expressed. Here was something she had managed to do. She was determined to be the best mother a child could have.

Her happiness and confidence began to return but, as the pregnancy progressed, Terry again managed to undermine these positive feelings. Lovingly he would inquire if she felt quite well. He would say she looked tired and suggest that she put her feet up and rest more. Rachel wondered if he thought her ankles looked swollen. He caringly bought her expensive facial products making her feel that her skin must look dull. He brought her gifts of wonderful herbal shampoos inferring that her hair had lost its shine.

Gradually, and not surprisingly, her bloom did go and she did feel bloated, tired and lethargic. She overheard him, on the telephone, tell people that she was having a difficult pregnancy and that she was run down and exhausted. Eventually all this became true.

It worried Rachel to see Terry rushing around seeing to everything as well as doing his job. He managed to make her feel guilty saying, "You stay where you are. I'll manage" in a long suffering tone. He called her "a poor thing". She felt pathetic and hopeless.

Rachel was well into her sixth month of pregnancy. She felt ugly and fat and useless. She recalled that morning – April 13th – Terry was rushing around as usual before going to school. "You lie on in bed, dear. Take it easy. I'll clear up all this mess when I get back and see to the washing. Don't you worry your pretty little head. I can cope." He kissed her forehead and off he went.

Rachel sighed, and settled back into the comfort of the pillows. Later after she had bathed and stared in the mirror at the sad reflection she made – swollen body, tired hair, dull skin – she sat down in front of the television. She was bored and so unhappy.

She had begun to have worrying thoughts that Terry might get fed up with her and begin to look elsewhere for a more attractive and more exciting, more capable companion. She was becoming tormented by this thought. Who could blame Terry if he strayed. It was all her fault.

She would have to make more of an effort. She decided that she would surprise him that night. She would dress up a bit. She'd put on some make up and do something with her hair. Firstly she would tidy up the house and do the washing.

For the first time in months she had a purpose, a plan. A sudden burst of energy moved her on. She was feeling better already. She worked enthusiastically around the house, tidying and cleaning. She popped a casserole into the oven. She slipped on a new maternity dress which Terry had chosen for her, tied a matching scarf around her blonde hair and added a touch of pink lipstick to her lips. She even managed to smile to herself in the mirror. She looked at the clock on the bedside table – just time to toss the washing into the machine, she thought. She filled her arms with the dirty linen and as she made her way to the top of the stairs she heard Terry's car pull into the driveway. "Oh dear" she said to herself, "I'll have to hurry." In her haste she caught her foot on a dangling towel and fell headlong down the stairs.

Terry opened the door and found his young wife lying at the foot of the stairs – various pieces of dirty laundry scattered all around her.

Rachel had failed again. She lost the baby. She could not even manage to be a mother. She felt worthless and hopeless and the grief she felt at the loss of her child was almost more than she could bear.

EIGHT

Mary Palmer did not have a telephone – she had no need of one. There was no one to call her and, if she had calls to make, she used the phone box in the high street, just a few yards down from the church. It seemed foolish but she felt safer, more anonymous, without a telephone.

She had explained her fears to her solicitor when she announced her intended change of identity. He alone knew who Rachel had become. He handled all her business but even he did not know where she lived. All correspondence he sent to a post office number and she collected it with the rest of her mail, every ten days or so. She rang him every week – he had insisted on that. His client, after all, was an extremely wealthy woman – having inherited all of her father's fortune when he died, less than four years before. Mary had an accountant and a financial advisor who worked with her solicitor. Money and material possessions meant little to Mary but she did appreciate the security that wealth gave to her. It was like a huge safety net. She could, if ever the need arose, pack up and run without considering any financial implications.

Had she been penniless and forced to live on state benefits or earn a living, her recovery and re-entry into the real world would have been much harder. She also realised that maintaining her anonymity would have been impossible if she had had to be computerised by officialdom.

Mary was fully aware of and grateful for the financial security left to her by her father. She was also aware that it was the presence of this vast fortune which was drawing her ex husband ever closer to her. She knew that, if it were not for the money, Terry would have forgotten all about her long ago.

A few days following the second newspaper article Mary had a scheduled appointment with her solicitor. She placed the relevant clippings into her handbag. She did not like the way they made her feel. It was as if she was carrying something offensive and unclean in her bag.

Mary's solicitor was Howard Hamilton. He had been a junior trainee with her father's solicitor. He had been summoned frequently by his senior to witness signatures on various documents and Mary had empathised with his lack of confidence and general unease on such occasions.

After Mary's father's death and the completion of all the complicated legalities she decided to find a new solicitor – a new beginning – distancing herself from lots of unhappy memories. She decided to seek out Howard Hamilton and was informed that he had joined a small legal firm as a junior partner, in another town, a few months before. This suited Mary very well. She needed to find him. He knew her history. She could not bear to start with someone new. There were, after all, many important decisions to be made and she desperately wanted a friendly face and a supportive, legal framework behind her.

This decision, one of the first she had to make as an independent wealthy woman, was a good one. Howard Hamilton had matured, grown into a fine, confident lawyer, but he had not forgotten how it had felt to be insecure and vulnerable.

On their first meeting he welcomed his new client warmly and with a great deal of sympathy and concern. He was pleased and relieved to see how well she looked. She bore little resemblance to the sad, pathetic being he had first encountered as she leant so weakly on her father's arm, while Howard witnessed her signatures on her divorce papers, all these years ago. He would never forget Rachel's pale waxen cheeks, her trembling hand on the pen, as she signed her name over and over again. She had been like a robot moving and doing as instructed – and her eyes – such empty, bewildered eyes. He remembered too, the gentle way her father treated her. This vibrant, charismatic, big man who had always seemed loud, determined and forceful was quiet and loving and fiercely protective of this fragile, broken girl – his beloved daughter.

When Rachel walked into his office that first day he scarcely recognised her. He had been recalling their last meeting and her sad history over the days prior to this reunion and remembering the distressing figure she had been.

She seemed taller. She was, of course, much older but she had a freshness and had lost her fragility. Her hair was darker and worn away from her face, gathered neatly at the back of her head. She wore tinted glasses and when she removed them her blue eyes looked straight into his with an almost unsettling directness and self assurance. Her eyes had no warmth or sparkle but they did indicate how very far she had progressed since last he saw her.

She held out an unadorned hand with long graceful fingers and returned his strong grip. "It is nice to see you again," she said in a deep harmonious voice.

He held out a chair for her in front of his heavy mahogany desk – it was incongruous in this modern office but it had belonged to Howard's grandfather and he loved it. It gave him a feeling of strength and depth and continuity.

"I was so sorry to hear about your father." He said quietly. "He was a fine man."

The woman opposite became a young girl again as her composure slipped for a moment and the blue eyes filled with tears. "Thank you." She said, "I miss him terribly!" She took an almost imperceptible deep breath and sat down, her momentary loss of balance restored.

Howard was filled with a deep admiration for this woman as he realised how great a personal loss the death of her father must have been. She had come to lean on him so completely. He had been her rock.

She was eager to get down to business. She produced a file of papers and a neat page of numbered notes she had prepared – it looked like an agenda for a board meeting. She was her father's daughter. She had prepared well for this meeting and wanted to be in charge of proceedings. He awaited her lead.

She swallowed and began. "I feel incredibly vulnerable now that my father has gone and I need to hide away and feel safe for a while. I need time to adjust and prepare myself for life in the world without him. Do you understand?" she asked hopefully.

"I think I do" Howard said gently. "What can I do to help?" He knew he did not understand. How could he! He had not suffered the way this woman had. He had not been where she had been.

"I plan to change my identity and go and live where no one will know anything about my past or my financial status." She continued, her voice steady and serious. "I feel that I need time to come to terms with everything and to find out who I really am and what I am here for, I suppose." These last words seemed to surprise her but she recognised their truth and a wry smile touched her lips. "From now on and on all my notes I want you to regard me as Mary Parker. I have found a house to rent in a small town within a fifty mile radius of here. I prefer that you do not know my address."

He made an attempt to protest but she continued, "This must seem ridiculous and out of all proportion but it is what I have decided and how I want things to be, for the time being. I have a fear, even a terror, that my ex husband may try to find me when he learns of my father's death. My expected inheritance was, after all, what attracted him to me in the first place. I am much stronger mentally now but not yet strong enough to face him."

The solicitor was beginning to understand where his new client was coming from. She was quite right. Terry Harrison would indeed be alert to the consequences of the recent death of the wealthy businessman and the resulting inheritance coming to his ex wife.

Rachel's father had been the huge powerful barrier erected between Rachel and Terry and now that protective barrier was no longer there. It was no wonder that his client felt vulnerable and afraid.

"Right!" Howard said "I'm beginning to understand. I'll do all I can to help you. I do feel concerned that you feel you have to keep your whereabouts hidden even from your solicitor but I will respect this if I must. You have obviously thought everything out very thoroughly."

The meeting then became more ordinary – business and legal

matters were discussed and Howard Hamilton felt back in control. He was an excellent solicitor and he loved his work and knew the law and the world of finance and business inside and out.

Mary knew that she had made the right choice with this man. She trusted and respected him. This was so important – he was, after all, the only person in the entire world who knew where Mary Parker had come from and where Rachel Oldfield-Harrison had gone!

As Mary was about to leave, Howard asked "Is there anything else, Mary?" He smiled at her as he tried out her new name.

"This may sound a bit paranoid.... I've been given many labels over the years but strangely enough paranoia was never one of them!" She made this comment almost as if she were speaking to herself, then continued, "You will make sure that my old name – Rachel Oldfield or Rachel Harrison – does not appear anywhere in your office. Not in the appointment book – not in the telephone memo file and not in the computer! You will have to make up some story for your secretary. It does sound as if I am not trusting you. I am sorry about that. It probably sounds melodramatic and a bit foolish but I do need you to do this for me."

"I will, I will, I promise!" Howard tried to reassure her. "Leave it to me and try not to worry!"

Over the subsequent months Howard Hamilton had become used to his strange, unconventional client. The arrangements insisted upon by the woman he now knew and thought of as Mary Parker, were working well. He had arranged for an accountant and financial advisor to help manage Mary Parker's investments and accounts. They used his office address for all correspondence with Mary. This was unusual but Howard explained that Mrs. Parker was not, as yet, settled in a permanent residence and preferred that all her business affairs were centralised at his office for the time being.

Over the months Howard saw changes in Mary. She continued to improve and to grow stronger. It was obvious that she was beginning to feel safe again. It was inevitable that they began to feel like friends. When two people share a secret a bond of trust and empathy grows. They relaxed with one another and very gradually they found that their conversations moved on from that of business to a sharing of anecdotes, descriptions of trivial events in one another's lives, onto subjects of literature, art and music. Howard was aware of the changes in their relationship but was sensitive to Mary's boundaries.

They both looked forward to their monthly meetings and Howard allowed extra time for her appointments in case they ran on. Eventually they extended over lunch time and he would arrange for coffee and sandwiches to be served.

When Mary entered Howard's office that day, with the press cuttings in her bag, he was aware of a change in her demeanour. She had lost her flowing relaxed way of moving – there was a slight tremble in her hand as she held it out to him in greeting and her mouth seemed tense and her smile forced. He could see that something was troubling her deeply but he said nothing. If she wanted to share her worry with him, she would do so when she felt ready.

He did not have long to wait. Mary was no sooner seated than she reached inside her bag and handed him the newspaper clippings, held out between thumb and forefinger as if contaminated with some deadly disease. "Did you happen to see these in the paper a week or so ago?" she asked.

Howard glanced quickly over the two cuttings then, without saying a word, he proceeded to read them again, carefully and mindfully as solicitors do. Legal people do not like to give quick answers. They seem to be thoroughly trained in the art of 'think before you speak'.

It was apparent to Mary that Howard had known nothing about these articles. She was encouraged by the serious way he was regarding them and she knew he was not about to undervalue the seriousness of their content. Above all, he was not going to tell her not to worry. He was the only person she could share this with and she desperately needed his support.

His eyes met hers. They were full of concern and compassion. "This must have been quite a shock for you," he said. "You should have contacted me sooner."

"I know, but I had to get my head around it first — deal with it in my own way — distance myself from it and then face it bit by bit. Do you understand?"

He could see what this blast from the past had done to her. He realised how alone she must feel and how she must be missing her father. A part of him wanted to get up from his seat behind the huge desk and touch her, tell her he would look after her and protect her and not to worry. Instead he asked "What do you think this means? What's going on?"

"I think – no I know – that Terry was behind the first article. He is trying to trace me. It's exactly what I was afraid of. He has heard about Daddy's death and he has decided that it is down to him to seek out and console the grieving daughter — help her to cope with her huge financial burden. Poor hopeless Rachel!" She smiled sadly and cynically. "As for the second article," she went on, "I would guess that someone, probably a close relative of the schoolgirl he ran off with, contacted the paper. They would have been infuriated by the portrait of Terry described in the earlier article. Whoever it was felt that I needed protecting from this man. How right they were!"

Howard nodded. "That sounds about right. There's been nothing else since?" His eyes scanned the newspaper clipping and he wrote down the dates from the top of the pages onto his pad.

"No, I've read every word in the paper every day since then and there has been nothing at all. But it's not over yet. Terry won't give up so easily. He's out there and he's getting closer. I can feel it." She shivered and he could sense her fear.

"You do know that he has no legal rights to anything? You have been divorced for a few years now." Howard knew, as he said this, that he was patronising his client. She was an intelligent woman and knew all of this. Mary did not seem to take offence. "Oh yes, I do know that. My fear is not that he will take my money – that I would not care about. My fear is that he may take my reason – my mind – as he did before. I know that I am no longer the person I was but I don't feel that I am ready to face that man again. This, after all, is why I have been hiding all this time. I feel angry with myself for allowing him to have this power over me. But I am working on this. I just need more time."

"What can I do to help?" Howard asked. His abilities as a lawyer seemed somehow inadequate.

"I don't know. I just want you to be extra vigilant. You and this office are the only link between myself and Rachel."

"Would you like me to locate Terry for you?" Howard asked. "I have a very good private investigator on my books."

This took Mary completely by surprise. This was something she had never considered, something she had never contemplated. She looked aghast and horrified. She forced air from between her lips in a long sigh, then said, "I'd never thought of that. Take the initiative, you mean. Oh I don't know. I'll have to give this some thought. Can I think about it and let you know?"

"Of course. It was only an idea. It is best not to make any rushed decisions. I have to say I think you are handling all of this extremely well. Let's have coffee now and talk about something else over lunch."

By the time Mary left the solicitor's office that afternoon she was feeling better. She felt less alone now that she had confided in someone.

Howard was feeling quite concerned about her. As they shook hands in farewell he said, "I do wish you would reconsider giving me a contact address or telephone number. Have you thought about having a mobile phone? No one could get your number unless you gave it to them. All you would have to do is buy a phone and the cards to go with it and of course give me your number. What do you say? You would be able to ring me at any time. You have all my numbers. Please say that you'll think about it?"

On her way to the train, Mary thought about Howard's suggestion. It did make sense. With an uncharacteristic impulsiveness she decided to buy a mobile phone before she returned home then she could ring Howard later and give him her number. He had been so kind and concerned about her it seemed the least she could do . He would be surprised and pleased to hear from her so soon. It did not seem fair to worry him by insisting on remaining incommunicado.

Later that evening she made her first call on her new phone. As she went to bed that night she felt that she had made another important step towards normality and her reconnection to the outside world. It was a link, even though it was only with one other person – it was one more than she had had that morning. As she wrote in her journal, she realised that already something positive had come about as a result of Terry's unwelcome reappearance into her life. She had, thanks to the newspaper articles, taken another significant step forward. She smiled to herself as she wrote, 'I can handle anything if I take it one step at a time'. She slept well that night – the best night she had had since her morning newspaper had contaminated her breakfast table.

Mary awoke early next morning and went for a long walk. Her mind was busy. She kept thinking about the suggestion Howard had made about locating Terry. Her stomach turned over whenever she thought of it and a tiny voice inside her begged, 'not yet – not yet!' She could see that employing Howard's private investigator would give her a feeling of being in control but her instinct was to leave well alone. By the time she had returned from her walk she had decided to follow her instinct and do nothing for the time being.

NINE

Three days later Mary was reading quietly on the patio, the grey cat curled on her knee, a glass of iced tea on the table nearby. She was feeling relaxed and contented. A strange sound disturbed the peacefulness. It was her mobile phone. Where had she left it? She hurried inside trying to locate the insistent high pitched sound. She found the phone beside her bed and hurriedly pressed a button – hoping that it was the right one. She had not received an incoming call before. She held the tiny piece to her ear and in a hesitant voice said, "Yes....?"

On the other end Howard's voice said, "I hope I haven't startled you. You won't be used to telephones ringing."

"You're right," she replied. "I don't know if I really like it. Perhaps I'm not ready for the modern world and its technology."

Howard continued, "I felt I had to ring you, Mary. Something has happened. It may be nothing to do with you but I thought I ought to let you know that we had a break in at the office last night. Nothing seems to have been taken but the filing cabinet has been forced open and the drawers in my desk have been ransacked. It does look as if someone was looking for something. It struck me that it might have something to do with Terry."

Mary went cold. An icy tingle ran down her spine and a huge hand seemed to claw at her solar plexus. She could not speak.

"Are you there? Are you OK, Mary?" Howard's voice was agitated. "He couldn't have found anything – even if it was him. There was nothing written down to connect you to Rachel and nothing to say where you are – because I don't know that – nobody does. You are perfectly safe."

"I know, I know, but somehow I don't feel very safe right now."

Mary managed to say. She had sunk heavily onto a chair in the corner of the bedroom. "Let me have some time to deal with this, Howard. I'll speak to you later. I'll be all right. Don't worry." She switched off the phone and tossed it aside – hating it for the news it had brought. She headed once more for the bench at the foot of the garden.

Mary had become calm and peaceful again as she went through her ritual of breathing, balancing and quieting. She stretched, took another deep breath and opened her eyes and smiled. A few yards away Tom was seated quietly with his back to her. How sensitive he was. He instinctively knew not to intrude. What an exceptionally beautiful child he was in every way, Mary thought to herself as she turned to speak to the little boy.

"Hello, Tom." Mary said and he turned towards her his eyes asking if she was all right, his mouth smiling, full of concern.

"Hi, Mary" he said, "I've got some news. I need to speak to you about it."

She could tell that he was worried about something. He had momentarily forgotten about it in his concern for her.

As usual they made there way inside for a drink and a chat. They didn't say anything until they were seated at the kitchen table, hot drinks and biscuits in front of them.

"Right, Tom" Mary said. "What's your news?"

"I think I may be going away – to boarding school, I mean." This was the first time he had put this into words and it was as if the enormity and the reality of the forthcoming event suddenly hit him. A look of horror and fear filled his face. "I don't want to go." He hadn't said that before either.

Mary did not say anything, just met his eyes and slightly moved her head, acknowledging the depth and strength of his emotions, responding to his feelings and allowing him a safe, accepting place in which to express and explore them.

The small boy accepted this gift from her. He took a long drink from the beaker of chocolate, then went on. "Daddy has gotten a new job in Borneo – that's a long, long way away. It's for two years and he and Mummy have decided that it's best if me and Cathy stay here and go to boarding school and see them only in the holidays. They will come to England at Christmas and Easter and we will go to Borneo in the long summer holidays. We have to spend half terms with Grandma or Auntie Chris in Yorkshire. It's all been decided!" He paused for a moment, a look of hopelessness in his eyes. That look of resignation that a child shows when choices are made for them and their opinions are not even considered.

"Cathy thinks it is all wonderful and exciting. I did too at first. But now I'm not so sure. I like things the way they are. Why do things always have to change?" He sighed heavily and gave Mary a crooked wry smile and waited for her to speak.

"Well, Tom. This is news, isn't it? It's no wonder you are feeling all mixed up. It is hard to deal with change of any kind and this is a big change and has come all of a sudden." Tom nodded. He was really listening – wanting help. "I find it best" Mary went on, "to deal with change very slowly – bit by bit, moment by moment. Don't look too far ahead and try not to worry about things that may never happen." She heard the advice that she was giving to Tom and realised it was well worth listening to.

"I'm really going to miss you, Mary, and Shadow. You will be able to keep her for me when I've gone? You'll explain to her where I am and that I haven't forgotten her?"

"Don't you worry, Tom" Mary said. "Shadow and I will look after each other until you come home again. We'll both miss you but won't we have lots to tell each other when you come back. I expect you'll make lots of new friends and have lots of adventures."

Mary was indeed going to miss this small boy. She loved his companionship and his quiet way of just appearing as if by magic. She felt a real ache in her heart as she thought of this sensitive child being sent to boarding school and being separated from his parents and the security of his home for so long. She felt sure that she would never have let her child go away. She sighed and had a sad far away look in her eyes. Tom moved over beside her. "Don't be sad, Mary" he said. "I'll visit you in the holidays and I can write to you and send you pictures. Will you write to me?"

"Of course I will. We'll be pen pals, shall we?"

"What's that?" he asked.

"It's the name you give to good friends who write to one another and share all their news so that it doesn't matter so much that they are apart."

"Great" said Tom smiling excitedly, "you and me will be pen pals!"

Two days later Mary met Tom's mother. "Tom tells me that you are going away. Borneo, is that right?" she inquired.

"Yes, it's all rather sudden. I don't know whether I am coming or going – what with schools, uniforms, injections, etc. to see to, as well as sorting out the house."

"You're not selling the house are you?" Mary asked. It was most unlike her to be so inquisitive.

"No, we've decided to let it. Someone has taken it for a twelve month lease – a young couple, new to the area. They want to see how they like it around here before they think about buying a property."

Mary's heart lurched. This was even worse than she and Tom had imagined. He would not be coming back next door even in the holidays. Tom, she felt sure, had been totally unaware of this possibility. He was going to be devastated.

Tom's mother must have been surprised to find her usually quiet neighbour so talkative. Mary continued, "Tom tells me that he and Cathy are going to boarding school. Is the school far from here?"

"Not too far, about forty miles. My sister and family and my mother live quite near and either of them can have the children for half terms and occasional weekends. It's all most convenient. I'm sure they'll love it. Well, I must dash. I have a million things to do!"

The woman from next door was gone – her mind already on name tags and inventories.

Mary was surprised at how deeply she felt the impending departure of the boy from next door. She felt bereft and abandoned and even wondered if she would want to stay here after he had gone. She felt confused and unsettled and when she wrote in her journal that day she found that she was extremely angry.

It took her several days and many pages to work through these emotions. The events of the last weeks had stirred up a lot of emotional garbage from the past and Mary, as she had learned, took her time to look at it all, analyse it and then release it. This type of inner work she found physically and emotionally exhausting and she felt tired and drained as a result.

While she had been focusing on the issues surrounding Tom she had thought less about the possible reappearance of her ex husband. However, she knew that that issue was pending – lying out of sight in her mental and emotional in-tray.

TEN

About a week later, as Mary sat, peaceably sketching by the river feeling very contented and relaxed, she noticed that thoughts of Terry kept coming into her mind. This, she thought, must be the right time to consider the Terry issue once more. She let her mind work slowly – allowing thoughts to drift in and out – not challenging them or fighting them – no mental arguments – just floating ideas and options drifting in and out like passing clouds in a summer's sky. It was as if she was more of an observer, some casual bystander. She was distanced emotionally from her thoughts. She continued her sketching and the corner of the river bank began to come alive on her paper – the way the sunlight hit the water, the reflections and the flowers and the grasses on the water's edge. Her pencil moved quickly, shading and cross hatching producing many subtle levels of tone and texture. Her eyes darted from the scene to the reproduction – her head remained still. Anyone watching would have thought that her entire being was totally focused on this activity.

Almost two hours later she quietly folded up her sketching pad – popped her pencils into her rucksack and made her way homewards across the fields. The grey cat, who had been chasing and stalking butterflies, joined her as she approached the gate into the rear garden.

Mary was still feeling controlled and relaxed. She made herself a sandwich and some tea and headed with it, balanced on a tray, towards the bench under the willow tree. She remained calm and mindfully ate and drank – savouring the experience.

She felt ready now to open up a little more – to allow her emotions to merge with her thoughts. It was rather like the way an artist adds a tiny touch of new colour to an existing blend in order to produce a subtle change of hue. Mary realised that all the work she had done, all the progress she had made over the preceding years were, in a way, preparing her for the final and greatest test of all – her graduation would be in facing and dealing with all this, mentally and emotionally. Her doctorate would be awarded when she could meet Terry, face to face, and be unaffected by him.

Mary knew that Terry could not and would not harm her physically – that was not his style. His intent would be to worm his way back into her life and then to mentally destroy her as he gradually eased away her confidence and self esteem, just as he had done all these years before. She was sure that Terry imagined himself taking care of her, making her totally dependent on him for every decision and, in this way, taking ultimate charge of her not insubstantial inheritance.

As she dealt with this image she shuddered and pulled her cardigan closer around her shoulders. A deep dread and disgust filled her being as she recollected the figure of the pitiable wretch she had once been – the puppet in Terry's hands. He had done this to her once and how sure was she that he could not do it to her again?

"Never! Never!" she said aloud, startling herself as she did so. She had pulled herself up straight – a look of determination on her face. She looked ready for a fight.

She could, if she chose to, arrange for Howard to locate Terry and pay him off. She was quite sure that her ex husband would readily agree to keep out of her life for a payment of several hundred thousand pounds but this, she knew, could never be an option. Her father would turn in his grave if he thought that Terry was to benefit by so much as one penny from her legacy. She recalled his satisfaction as she signed the divorce papers and how he had opened the best champagne to celebrate the arrival of her decree absolute.

"He's out of your life forever now, Rachel. You can go on from here and rebuild a life for yourself. You never have to lay eyes on that low life again. This is a great day for both of us." He'd walked over and hugged her close. "Everything is going to work out fine. Just you wait and see!"

Mary's eyes misted as she relived this memory of her father. She could still feel the warmth of his strong arms around her and the touch of his lips as he spoke kindly into her ear. How she missed him still.

"No. He won't get a penny. I'll show him! I'll make you proud of me, Daddy!" she said under her breath.

She had made up her mind. She knew that until she had stood in front of Terry and told him that he was no longer welcome anywhere in her life and that she had shown him how mentally strong she had become, she would not be able to put the past behind her. She needed to do this. Once it was done she would be able to come out of hiding and move on and take control of her life.

It was two days later when Mary made her way once again into Howard's office. She was looking forward to sharing her feelings about Terry with him and the decisions she had made.

They had not spoken since the incident of the break-in and Howard had a concerned look in his eyes when they met.

"How are you?" he said as he held out his hand to her. This was not just a casual greeting. He was genuinely inquiring as to her state of mind and physical well being.

"I'm fine," she answered, meeting his gaze. "I really am. Don't worry. It's not been easy but I have coped and I've done a lot of thinking these last few weeks."

Howard was called to the outer office and as Mary sat alone in the familiar office she suddenly shivered as her eyes fell on a tall grey filing cabinet in the far corner of the room. Had Terry stood there and perhaps touched the file with her name on it? But he did not know her name. Was there anything at all in this office with a mention of her former name – the name he would recognise? She had to know.

When Howard returned he noticed her serious expression and guessed what she was thinking.

"After the break-in" he said "I went through all of your paperwork – just in case, just to make sure. And I honestly cannot see how anyone could make a connection between Mary Parker and who you used to be. Nothing, that is, apart from the fact that you are a female and the dates when we started representing you. There is, of course, the fact that you have no address – only the post office number. That does set your file apart from the others. But that is all. Would you like to take a look at your file and check for yourself?"

"No, I'll take your word for it. Do you think that I am over reacting and that this break-in has nothing whatsoever to do with my ex husband?"

"No I don't. In fact there is something else I have to tell you."

Mary held her breath as the tall slim man in front of her continued.

"Last night I attended a retiral party for old Matthews, your late father's solicitor. I was seated next to Muriel – you remember Muriel? She was personal assistant and right hand to your father's solicitor?" Mary nodded eager for him to get on with what he had to tell her. "She, of course, has no idea that I am acting for you but your father's name came up in conversation and she mentioned that a couple of months ago a gentleman had been in trying to trace any surviving relatives of your father. He said that he was an old friend and had been out of the country for several years and had only just heard of your father's death. She had, of course, been unable to give him any information apart from the fact that the firm no longer acted for any of the heirs. He had asked to speak with Mr. Matthews but that had not been possible as he was out of town for a few weeks. I didn't want to appear too interested but I did ask if the man in question was of a similar age to your father and she gave me a rough description. He was, she thought, in his early to middle fifties – slim built, though thickening a bit around the middle. His hair was greying but was still dark – he wore glasses and had a soft, pleasant voice with no evidence of an accent. She had I could tell taken quite a shine to him!

He had apparently asked her out to lunch but she had explained that she couldn't leave the office that day and was lunching in. He had insisted on returning later with a picnic meal for both of them and it was over lunch that he had spoken more of his sadness at the loss of his friend and his need to find Rachel. He knew that she had been ill for a long time and had been in a convalescent home when he had last spoken to her father. He now felt compelled to track her down and visit her and offer her his heartfelt condolences.

'He was such a nice man', Muriel told me. She told him that she would see if she could find out anything from me, or any of the other partners. I was surprised to hear that my name had been mentioned and said so. Muriel said that he was just showing an interest in the practice – asked if all the names on the letterhead were still with the company – things like that. She had happened to mention that I had left a year or so ago. He thought he remembered me and wanted to know where I had gone. She hoped I did not mind but she had given him my new address."

It was obvious to Howard that this was indeed Terry Harrison and that he knew exactly how to handle women. He was a charming con-man with exceptional manipulative powers.

Mary's face had lost all of its colour and her lips were pressed tightly together as she listened to this account from Howard. Her fingers were clenched as they gripped the arms of the chair. She did not need to speak. Her reaction was clear to see. Howard got up and handed her a glass of water and laid a comforting hand on her shoulder.

"Are you all right, Mary?" Howard asked, his voice full of concern.

"Just give me a few minutes," Mary said and she got up from the chair, placed the glass of water on top of the desk, and moved to an arm chair at the other end of the spacious office. She sat on the front of the cushion, her feet side by side, firmly positioned on the thick carpet and closed her eyes.

Howard watched her discreetly from behind his desk. She took a deep breath and let it out very slowly and quietly. She repeated this a few times and each time he could see a change occurring – a peacefulness came over her. At last she stretched her arms above her head – looked up and smiled and opened her eyes. She turned towards Howard and covered him in the warmth of her smile as she said, "Sorry about that. It's a routine I do to de-stress myself. I don't usually do it in public. I have more subtle methods for such occasions but this was a bit of an emergency and I knew you would understand!"

"You never cease to amaze me, Mary. Shall we have some coffee now?"

"Thank you. That would be great. I need a little time before we go on. I need to digest all that you have told me. As you know I am not one who makes hasty decisions." She laughed.

As they sipped their drinks Howard told Mary about a new play he had been to see recently. She was familiar with the play-wright but did not know this latest production.

Mary finished her coffee, put the cup carefully onto the saucer and said, "Right, back to business. What next?"

"I don't know" Howard said. He smiled and remarked, "I'm a great believer in the saying, 'when in doubt, do nowt'!"

" I've given this a lot of thought," Mary said. "I even considered having you find Terry and paying him off. But that seems like a coward's way out as does running away again. This, I know, is a challenge the Universe has set me. In a way I know that if I can deal with this I will know for certain that I have conquered my illness and can move on at last. Do you know I don't have an up to date passport or even a current driving license because of him. I didn't want my name and address on anything. I've lived in fear for too long. This is the highest hurdle so far but I think that I am almost ready to face it."

"Almost?" he said lifting his eyebrows questioningly.

"Yes" she smiled. "Not yet but soon. I need a little more time. It's funny, but a part of me is intrigued and wants to wait and see what Terry will do next. He won't give up. I do know that. He thinks that I am his winning lottery ticket – the one which he has somehow misplaced but not lost."

"I think you are right. He has somehow convinced himself that you are connected with me. He may or may not know that you are Mary Parker. I suppose he could hang about outside my office, day after day, and watch my clients come and go, or he may even hire someone to look for you."

Mary nodded, "I do feel I want to be in control of where and when and how I meet Terry. I couldn't bear it if it was unexpected and I was taken off guard and unprepared. Perhaps I do need to seek him out just so that I know where and what he is up to. One thing for sure, I am glad that you talked me into having this mobile phone. You do keep yours turned on all the time?"

"Yes I do. So don't worry. You can reach me any time. You mustn't hesitate to ring me about anything."

"I'm going to take a few days just to sort things out in my mind. I'll give you a ring after that," she said as she rose to her feet and picked up her bag and the file of documents. "I bet you're glad you don't have too many clients like me!" she said as she left the office.

As Mary left the solicitor's building she could not help looking round. Was there someone watching, perhaps taking photographs of everyone who left this particular doorway? Was she being over dramatic and a touch paranoid? She pulled her woollen jacket close to her and hurried towards the bus stop. 'All is in perfect order,' she told herself. She affirmed that this was so but she did not quite manage to believe it. She took a seat at the back of the bus and found herself observing the cars behind – making sure that no one particular vehicle was following.

The uneasy feeling was still with Mary as the bus approached her destination. Mary disembarked about a mile from her usual stop, deciding to walk the final part of her journey. No one else alighted from the vehicle much to her relief and by the time she reached home she was feeling more confident that, for the time being at least, Terry was not too close. Even if he now was looking for Mary Parker he still did not know where she lived.

ELEVEN

Mary was diverted from her own problems soon after she arrived home. When she had thrown off her shoes and had a cup of tea, she decided to spend some quiet time in her little room upstairs. She had selected the kind of music she needed and was about to sit back and enjoy it when her attention was caught by the picture from her window of a small boy huddled beside a grey cat in the corner of the garden. Tom was having a deep and very earnest conversation with the ever obliging Shadow. Shadow was sitting sphinx like and Tom was pouring out his emotions to his silent listener. Client and counsellor – Mary smiled to herself. This brought back memories. Shadow, she felt, would probably have been more useful than many of the counsellors she had come across over her years of therapy.

Tom had come round looking for Mary that afternoon but had found the house next door locked up. He was upset and unhappy and needed someone to talk to. He was just about to leave when he noticed Shadow on the rockery, almost invisible against the grey stone and the dark wall behind.

"Hi, Shadow!" Tom said "Mary's out, is she?" He crouched down and stroked the soft fur. Shadow looked at him and nudged his hand with the side of her head in welcome. Tom tickled her ears and she began to purr.

Tom sat down on the large stone next to the cat and they sat quietly for a while both deep in thought. Then Tom spoke.

"I'm going away to-morrow and I won't be coming back for a very long time." The words caught in his throat and a tear began to move down his cheek. He didn't seem to notice it. His hand kept stroking the cat and her purr was steady and rhythmical and very comforting. "They're sending me off to boarding school." he continued in a resigned, hopeless sort of voice. "I know that I will hate it and if I do, I shall run away. That's what I am going to do. Don't tell anyone, Shadow. I've already made plans and I have saved up some money. People are feeling sorry for me and they keep giving me money to buy something. Well I am saving it all." He went quiet again for a while then said, "The worst thing of all is we won't even be able to come back here in the holidays. Our house is being rented out for two years. I can't bear it. I won't have my bedroom and all my things.

I won't have the garden and the fields and the river and worst of all, I won't have you or Mary!" A huge sob escaped and the grey cat moved closer and onto his knee. "I tried to tell Mummy and Daddy how I was feeling but they just said not to be so silly and that two years would soon pass and that I'd be too busy enjoying all the new exciting things to miss this old place and I'd soon forget all about it – but I won't! I know I'm just going to hate boarding school. I just know! I asked if I could come here and stay with you and Mary sometimes but they said, no. I heard them talking about it one night and they said that they couldn't really allow it as they knew nothing at all about Mary. They said she could be a child abductor or anything! And they laughed...! That was an awful thing to say about Mary, wasn't it? She is the nicest, kindest person in the whole world.

Oh I wish I could stay here with you. I hate Mummy and Daddy. I really do!"

Mary left the quiet sanctuary and the haunting music and made her way into the garden. This could wait. She had the feeling that Tom was in need of some human contact. Shadow had played her part but now Mary knew she had a contribution to make.

As the patio door opened two heads turned towards the tall woman. Tom was on his feet and running towards her, "Oh. Mary, you're back. Thank goodness! I thought you had gone away and I wouldn't be able to say goodbye." He launched himself at her and hugged her. This had never happened before. Her arms moved instinctively around the small sobbing child.

"Oh, Tom!" she said "Oh, Tom! It's all right. I'm here now." She drew him with her onto the bench on the patio and let him cry. Inside she sobbed too. She knew this feeling, this despair, this pain, this heartbreak – she remembered it. All the arms which had held her had never given her what she needed. Terry's had made her feel a failure. Nurses and professional carers had made her feel like a bag of symptoms. And her father had felt totally impotent and broken and helpless.

What she gave Tom was her total love and compassion and acceptance. She couldn't fix it – she couldn't change anything – she could only be there and love him and this she did totally, non judgementally and unconditionally.

Gradually the sobs began to subside and the small boy, exhausted and spent, went limp. He seemed even smaller. They did not speak – just sat very still and very close. There are no words for times like these – our vast language does not have the right vocabulary.

Some time later Tom stirred and looked up into Mary's face.

"Shall we have a drink now?" she said gently.

"Yes, hot chocolate with sprinkles. Can I make it, Mary?" Tom was on his feet.

"I think I'll have tea, Tom. Let's put the kettle on."

When they were settled in their usual places at the kitchen table with their respective drinks and a plate of biscuits, Tom was ready to share his troubles with Mary. He confided in her. He told her of his fears, his anger and his despair. He did not tell her of his plans to run away and he did not tell her what he had overheard his parents say about her. These were his secrets – only shared with a silent, grey feline who could be trusted not to blab!

Mary instinctively knew how to honour the child's feelings. She offered him no platitudes, no cliches and no promise of a happy ending. These were Tom's feelings – his emotions —- and she respected them and honoured them as such. She was aware that so often well meaning people try to negate or dilute such feelings. Sometimes this may be appropriate but Tom, she knew, had not come to her to be told that everything would be all right and not to worry. He wanted more from her than this.

Mary knew that what she said to this small, unhappy boy had to be meaningful and useful to him. She chose her words carefully – speaking to him not as a child but as a human being, someone who was deeply troubled finding himself in a scary place in a not too friendly world. She knew this terrain, she remembered its loneliness, she recalled its emptiness and she felt his fear!

"Tom," she said "I can see that this is a very unhappy time for you. You must be feeling a bit scared and uncertain at all these changes. In the past and even now, when I start to worry about things, I find it helps if I try to stay in the moment – not look ahead and anticipate what may or may not lie ahead. Live, not even one day at a time – more one hour at a time – even less if needs be. Take this moment, for example, we are enjoying each other's company. This is a wonderful moment – enjoy it. Hold these special moments inside. I do this and sometimes when I am having a moment which isn't so good, I can go back inside myself and enjoy such a moment, or another like it, instead. When I am at the dentist, for example, I imagine that I am by the river sketching, or on top of a mountain or in my room upstairs listening to music. No one can ever take away your special moments or change them. So, when life seems all upside down and back to front and everything is changing, keep taking out your special moments and reliving them. That's what I do and, when you are away at school and I am missing you, I will close my eyes and relive one of our special moments together. Do you think you might be able to try that, Tom? Perhaps we could think of a symbol or ceremony – a secret signal that reminds us of our special moments. Then, if either of us is missing the other, we can use it to switch on a memory."

Tom's eyes lit up, "Oh yes. That would be neat. Like a secret password or something?"

"How about a special scent? I have my little bottles of aromatherapy oils. We could choose one that we both like and you could take some away with you in a little bottle. If you put a touch on your wrist every morning you can have the scent handy whenever you need it. I can do the same."

"Yes, yes. Can we do it right now? Can we, Mary?" Tom was on his feet dancing excitedly, his misery of a short time ago gone.

They went upstairs and spent a while sniffing and rejecting various aromas. There was much laughter as Tom expressed his opinions of the smell of some of the oils most graphically. Eventually, after much deliberation and hilarity, they both agreed on the delicate scent of lavender oil. Mary prepared a small bottle for the boy to take away with him mixing the fragrant essential oil in a carrier oil. They then found a special sticker to go on the bottle and Mary wrote on the bright label, 'For Special Moments – sniff as required!" She smiled to herself hoping that anyone reading it would not think it was some mood enhancing drug. Tom was delighted with it and insisted that Mary had an identically labelled bottle of her own.

"I'm not going to let anyone see this." he said. "This is our own special secret, Mary."

He left soon afterwards, clutching the bottle in one hand and promising to call in to say a final goodbye to Mary and Shadow the next morning. They were leaving after lunch.

That evening Mary settled down to read but found herself unable to concentrate. Her mind kept going back to Tom and the ordeal he was facing. She was extremely concerned for her small friend. She did not feel he had the mental toughness required for boarding school. In some ways he was mature for his years but in other ways he had that gentle naivety which would single him out from the other children. He was easily hurt and would be vulnerable, she felt, to bullying. She ached inside and wished that there was more she could do to help. She got up, after a while, and went over to her desk. She pulled out a packet of envelopes and a notepad. Carefully she addressed six envelopes to herself and put a stamp on each one. This was the first time she had written this address under her name – Mary Parker, Orchard Cottage, Main Street, Ashtonbury. She stared at it. Somehow it seemed to give her an identity and she liked the feeling. She had emerged from hiding and taken another step forward into the world. It was only a small thing but to Mary, in that moment, it seemed like a giant step. "Thank you, Tom!" she said as she gathered the envelopes and notepad ready to give to him next day. Inside the notepad she wrote, 'Write to me, Tom. Find special moments and tell me about them. I will send you some of mine.' She drew a quick sketch of herself, Tom and Shadow by the fish pond. At the top of the page she wrote out her mobile phone number. She could do no more.

She put everything inside a large brown envelope and wrote 'Tom' on the outside. Mary decided that she had better have something for Cathy too and inside a similar envelope she put some pretty notelets and a pen. She felt sure that Cathy would have plenty of people to write to.

As Mary went to bed that night she had a heavy feeling in her solar plexus. She knew that she had taken on some of Tom's pain. She lifted down the bottle of lavender oil with its individual label, opened it and put a touch of the oil onto her wrist. As she closed her eyes she sniffed the delicate scent and, in that instant, it was as if she and Tom were sitting in the summer meadow sketching together – the sky was blue, the air soft and fresh – a bee buzzed by and life was a joy. She had managed to bottle that moment.

Next day, just before noon, Tom and Cathy arrived to say their goodbyes. Cathy was wearing her new uniform as only she could. She modelled it to perfection and could have come straight from an American yearbook. She was full of confidence and excitement. Tom, on the other hand, looked ill at ease in the brand new clothes and his whole body said how much he hated them. He was putting on a brave face but Mary could see how he was feeling and her heart went out to him. He went off to stroke Shadow as Cathy prattled on nineteen to the dozen, unable to keep still.

Mary went inside and picked up the two envelopes she had prepared for the children. "Don't open them until later, when you are settled in at school," she said as she handed them over. They both thanked her politely and were gone. Tom looked back over his shoulder at Mary and gave a watery smile. Mary lifted her wrist and sniffed it and Tom followed the gesture and grinned.

The picture of that small boy in his neat new uniform stayed with Mary all day long. She was crying inside for him. How she hoped he would be happy at boarding school. 'Let people be kind to him', she prayed but there was a huge weight inside her heart that told her that this would not be so.

Mary was almost going through a period of grieving for her young friend from next door. She kept expecting to see him around the garden or in the field beyond or suddenly appearing through the patio doors. There was no other source of human comfort for her and she had to admit she missed it.

A few days after Tom had left she called at the house next door. This was something she had never done in the past and had never had any intention of doing. However she wanted news of Tom, the address of the school and to find out when his parents were leaving for Borneo.

Tom's mother was surprised to see Mary when she came to the door but she held it open inviting Mary to step inside. "Excuse the confusion. Isn't packing just the worst job? We leave at the end of the week and there is still masses to do. It's easier now that the children have gone. They're not under my feet all the time."

"How are they?" Mary inquired. "Have they settled in all right?"

"Oh yes. I'm sure they have. It's a marvellous school – an excellent reputation. We've had no emergency phone calls at least. Cathy was as happy as could be when we left. Tom was a bit tearful – but he'll soon get the hang of it I'm sure. He can be a bit of a baby. It'll toughen him up, his father says."

Mary cringed inside when she heard this. She could just hear Tom's father saying, "It'll make a man of you. No tears now, old son!"

Mary said, "Tom was anxious that I kept him informed about Shadow, his cat, and I promised to write to him. Could I possibly have the address of the school?"

Tom's mother looked surprised, "That's very good of you but won't it be a nuisance for you?"

"Not at all. Tom and I have become good friends. I shall miss his cheery face."

Tom's mother handed her a card with the details of the school printed on it. Mary thanked her and said, as she headed for the door, "I hope you will be able to bring Tom to see me and Shadow when you are back in the country. Will that be for Christmas?"

"We will have to see," said Tom's mother. "We will be spending Christmas with my mother in York. Thank you for coming round."

"Have a good journey," Mary said as she left clutching the card in her hand, knowing that the woman next door would have forgotten her visit by the time she closed the door.

When she was safely back inside Mary sat quietly for a while. She did not feel heartened by her visit next door and she needed to distance herself mentally from the woman who was Tom's mother, before she could write her letter to the home-sick little boy.

She moved to the piano and sat with a straight back on the antique carved stool. She let her fingers run over the keys – the music at first was loud and aggressive but slowly, as the minutes passed, it eased in tempo and became more gentle and passive before it became haunting and mystical. The expression on Mary's face and the set of her shoulders altered as the spirit of the music changed. When her fingers became still, a peaceful harmony filled the pianist and her living space.

She lifted the pad of note-paper and her pen and began to write.

'My Dear Tom, I have just enjoyed a special moment. I sat at the piano and let the music carry me away. I remember how you used to sit quietly while I played. I do miss you and I think of you all the time.'

She stopped writing and began to draw – a beautifully crafted pen drawing of herself at the piano and a small boy curled up in a big armchair with a cat on his knee. 'I will write again soon.' the letter continued 'From Your Special Pen Friend, Mary.'

She read what she had written. She was not satisfied with her effort but did not know if she could do better. She sighed frustratedly and popped the sheet of note paper into an envelope, wrote Tom's name and the address of the school onto the envelope and stuck on a first class stamp. She went out straight away to post it before she changed her mind.

TWELVE

That afternoon Mary made herself busy in the garden. She liked this time of year when things were slowing down. The cutting back of plants and tidying up ready for the approach of winter was satisfying. It had a sense of completion and order.

It was cold and damp but she worked quickly and energetically and kept herself warm. The light was beginning to go when she finished and she was feeling better as she cleaned up and went inside to feed an impatient hungry cat. She started as the phone rang out shrilly. This was still such a rare occurrence that it made her jump. She hurriedly picked up the tiny hand set and said, "Hello".

"It's Howard here." The familiar voice sounded in her ear. "I'm just ringing to see how you are!"

"I'm all right," she said. "I've just come in from the garden. I've been tidying up. It's done me good – very therapeutic – very grounding!"

"Have you had any further thoughts on the Terry business?" he asked.

"No, I can't say I have." Mary went on to explain about her concerns for Tom and how upset he had been. She had spoken to Howard before about her closeness to the child next door and he understood. Mary was so glad to have someone to share this with. She realised how bereft she was of human contacts, let alone friends.

"Something did strike me about Terry," she went on. "I was wondering if he might stake out my post office collection point, rather than your office. He'll expect me to pick up my mail regularly and it is only open in the mornings, so he wouldn't be so tied up keeping watch."

"That's true." Howard agreed. "Is there a way round that?"

"The only idea I can come up with is if I send you the card. You could collect my mail and readdress it to me here! As long as you don't write this address down anywhere, that should be fine."

"Yes, that would be an answer. Even if he recognises me it wouldn't matter. You feel you can trust me with your address now?"

"Of course. It was never a lack of trust in you. It was just the fear of having my address on file anywhere – and I was right, wasn't I?"

"You were." He laughed. "Now give me your address – I hope it isn't too complicated, if I have to remember it."

She gave him the address and she repeated it a couple of times.

"I'll send you the details of where and how to collect my mail – once a week is quite often enough – even less often really as you will be able to send most of it directly from your office. I don't get much else of any importance, apart from financial stuff! Well, thank you, Howard. I do appreciate this. I have to confess I was quite paranoid when I left your office last time. I kept looking over my shoulder and I haven't been near the sorting office. It's all getting a bit out of hand."

"Right, Mary, we'll speak again soon. Take care." Howard hung up.

Mary felt better after this call. It was so good to have someone to talk to — someone who knew all there was to know and who seemed to understand. She had been well guided when she chose Howard Hamilton as her solicitor. He was beginning to feel more like a friend – if she could remember what it felt like to have a friend!

Later that evening when Mary wrote in her journal she commented on how far she had progressed over the recent months. First of all she had opened up to the wide open spaces, the hills and the fields and the river. Next she had allowed herself to become attached to her garden and her home. She had then opened her heart to the small boy next door and in turn to the cat he had brought and entrusted to her care. Now she had opened up sufficiently to trust Howard with her address and to be open to telephone communication on her mobile phone.

She smiled to herself. Normal people would think nothing of

these things but, to her, these were all massive steps on her way back to normality. "You've done really well!" She wrote this message to herself in her journal. She had learned the great value of self worth. It had been a long hard struggle and now she could honour the work she had done and the achievements she had made.

Mary was surprised the following week when the postman delivered a large bundle of mail through her letterbox. Howard had forwarded the letters from her post office box as promised. There was also a letter addressed in her own handwriting – it was from Tom. She ignored the other post and quickly tore open the light blue envelope and pulled out the sheet of paper from inside. Her whole body was tense and excited. Tom had written only a few lines and had drawn a picture on the back.

> 'Dear, Mary,' the letter said, 'thank you for your present and for your letter. I liked the drawing very much. I miss you and Shadow very much. I don't like it here. It is very noisy and there is a funny smell Mummy and Daddy were here last week. They have gone away now. I wish I was at home with you. Write again soon. Love Tom, your pen pal.'

The picture he had drawn was labelled — his bed and those of five other children — a bedside chest of drawers and a small wardrobe next to each bed. His bed was next to the window. There was a stain on the paper. He had circled it and labelled it - 'a tear drop fell here.'

Mary's eyes filled with tears and her heart ached for her small friend forced to cry himself to sleep in this overcrowded room. Even children need their own space and privacy and Tom, she knew, needed it more than most.

Mary wrote back to Tom straight away. She did him another drawing. This special moment was of the two of them leaving the pet shop laden with things for a new kitten. That had been such a happy event – reliving it she hoped would remind Tom of it and lift his spirits, if only for a moment. She enclosed, with the letter, some stickers she had bought for him – all of different cats doing silly things. He could stick them on his books. She went out straight away to post this urgent letter. It was all she could do – it seemed so little.

When Mary returned she sat down and reached for the large envelope containing all her mail from her post office box. She tipped out the letters onto the kitchen table. At first glance they looked very dull but her attention was caught by a bright white envelope – it looked like a greetings card. Howard must have popped it in for her. She reached for it – the writing did seem familiar. She opened it smiling. The smile disappeared when she saw that it was a birthday card. It had been her birthday a few days before but no one knew who she was, let alone when her birthday fell. No one, that is, except Terry. He had tracked her down. He now knew that she was Mary Parker – he had found the post office number from Howard's files.

Mary felt sick. It was almost as if she had been abused or violated in some way. She opened the card – there was a verse but no signature. But she knew..... without a shadow of doubt, she knew. The picture on the front of the card was of a young couple punting on a river under hanging willow trees. She and Terry had gone punting in the very early days of their relationship. This was confirmation if she had needed any.

She had to speak to Howard. Tell him about the card. She reached for the phone and dialed his number. He answered straight away. She heard him excusing himself. He had a client with him.

"I'm sorry." Mary said. "Is this an awkward time? Shall I ring back?"

"It's O.K. Mary. Has something happened?"

"The letters you forwarded to me. They arrived this morning. I've just opened them and there is a birthday card from Terry! He knows who I am!"

Howard was obviously surprised, "That white envelope. I did wonder about that one, but I never dreamt..... What did he say on the card?"

"Nothing. It was unsigned. But I know it is from him. He's the only person who would know it was my birthday and the picture on the front is relevant to our past. I feel sick, sort of violated. I just had to talk to someone – share it, you know?"

"I understand. You were right to phone. Now there is no need to panic. Nothing has really changed. He only knows your box number. He is still only guessing that you are Mary Parker. He has no way of finding out where you live. You are quite safe."

"Yes, I know that. I'm feeling better already. Thank you, Howard. I'll go now and let you get on. Speak to you soon."

She did feel better. Howard was right. Nothing had changed. She had known all along that Terry had been the intruder in Howard's office and that he was getting ever closer.

She took a few deep breaths and began to look through the rest of her mail.

THIRTEEN

Terry Harrison had picked up some unsavoury skills in the short time he had spent in prison. He had been fortunate in being sent to an open prison. His barrister had spoken most eloquently on his behalf, telling the court of the unfortunate state of his marriage, the tragic loss of his unborn son and the severe pressures of caring for a sick wife.

On being released from prison Terry had left the country for several years. He was glad to be back in his own surroundings once more. He had been pleased with the time and effort he had devoted to the solicitor's personal assistant – Muriel, she had been called. He had not lost his touch and his instincts were as good as ever. He felt sure that Howard Hamilton was the key to his search for his ex wife. Rachel, had obviously decided to change her solicitor after the death of her father and she would have been likely to choose someone who already knew her history. She would have been more comfortable dealing with a familiar face.

He decided that it would not be a good idea to use the same approach with this solicitor's female staff. He would instead try out another skill – breaking and entering. He had not done this before but he felt confident that he could do it without being caught. He had a buzz of excitement as he made his plans.

He was surprised at how easy it all was. The security system was, he had to admit, fairly basic and his cell mates had taught him extremely well.

Once inside he found a door clearly marked with Howard Hamilton's name. He made his way to the large grey filing cabinet and had it unlocked in a matter of seconds. He quickly looked for a file marked with Rachel's name. There was nothing listed under either Oldfield or Harrison. She must have changed her name. He began the painstaking task of looking at every female file and again drew a blank. The only Rachel listed was an elderly widow, a resident in a local nursing home.

Terry was undeterred. He was certain that the person who had been his wife was hidden amongst these names. He began again, looking closely at the personal details of every female client. He laid aside any which seemed a possible match. When he had reached the end of the alphabet he had ten files on one side. Now he began to read these at greater length discarding each one as more information was revealed. It was a time consuming job.

Eventually he came to one, a lady called Mary Parker – she had been with the practice the right length of time and there seemed evidence of substantial funds. The most intriguing factor was that there was no telephone number and only a post office box number as an address. This was most peculiar. He nodded his head – "Gotcha!" he muttered. "Mary Parker, I know who you really are!"

But that was all that he knew. Still it was the start he needed. He made a note of the post office number and left the office delighted with his night's work!

As Terry was reading the daily paper a few days later, his eye fell on the date printed at the top of the page – October 18th. The following day would be Rachel's birthday. "I'll send her a card." he smiled to himself. He would not need to sign it. She would guess who had sent it. He would send it to Mary Parker at her box number. Rachel could change her name and hide herself away but she would still have the same birthday. She could not change that.

Terry took considerable time in the local newsagents choosing the most appropriate card for his ex wife. He wanted the picture to be meaningful – have a hidden message. When he picked up the card with the summer scene and the young lovers punting on an English river underneath the swaying willows, he knew that he had found the right card. This card would hold a special memory for the woman who had been such a young, carefree lover all these years ago.

He could recall that happy, idyllic time when he had courted and captured the beautiful, young heiress. It had all gone horribly wrong. If she hadn't lost the baby – that was when it all turned sour and he lost control. How differently it might have turned out.

Still it might not be too late. He was very hopeful that he could turn the clock back – push back the years. He and Rachel could build a life together again and this time there would be no interfering father, lurking in the background, to spoil things. He knew that he could handle Rachel. She had always been putty in his hands. He was sure that, once she got over the shock of seeing him again, she would realise that she needed him in her life.

He posted the card with a first class stamp and hoped she would collect her mail before too long. He had found out where the post office sorting office was situated in the town where Howard Hamilton had his practice. It was open Monday to Saturday from 7.30a.m. until 11.30a.m. He had decided to watch the doorway and see if he could catch a glimpse of Rachel as she collected the mail addressed to the mysterious Mary Parker.

Terry was working as an insurance salesman and he could easily juggle his hours to allow for this. He could even do some paperwork as he sat in his car.

The sorting office was beautifully positioned for his purpose. It was tucked in behind a row of shops at the edge of a large pay and display car park. It was possible for Terry to obtain a key position where he could view the doorway and the front desk without his car looking out of place or conspicuous.

Terry had learned about patience over the years and in all his money making schemes he had had to prepare the way and then await the ultimate pay off. The task of finding Rachel was, he felt, coming together rather well and he was confident of a successful and speedy conclusion.

On the third morning Terry noticed a car he had seen before pulling in in front of the sorting office. It was a beautiful car – a classic M.G. sports model in a startlingly, bright yellow. He had seen it parked in the reserved parking bay outside Howard Hamilton's office. A man in his early to mid forties, dressed in a smart suit, hurried into the post office building where he collected a bundle of mail.

"Damn it!" Terry muttered, "He's collecting Rachel's mail!" He had been wasting his time!

Over the next week or two Terry, whenever he had time to spare, kept an eye out for the yellow sports car. He was able to learn some of the habits of Rachel's smart young solicitor but he did not lead him any closer to the secret address. Terry was, for the time being, at a loss but he would bide his time and wait.

FOURTEEN

It was about three days after the arrival of the unwelcome birthday card. Mary was finding that her thoughts seemed to flow from her anxieties regarding the possible activities of her ex husband as he struggled to locate her and her deep concerns for the little boy from next door who, she was convinced, was going through his own personal hell all on his own.

Mary tried to keep busy – she continued to tidy up the garden and she cleaned the house from top to bottom. Her music was loud and upbeat as she tried to silence her mind and her painting had, for the time being, lost its delicate, gentle quality. She painted in wild contrasting colours – big abstract pictures expressing the turmoil in her mind. She still found deep quietness and calm in her meditation practice and she thanked heaven for her ability to use this even when she was so deeply troubled.

That night she was awakened from a deep sleep. Suddenly she was wide awake – her heart was racing and all was absolutely silent. There was not a sound to be heard. She sat up, switched on her bedside light and looked at the clock. It was only a quarter to three. What had disturbed her? Had she been dreaming? Shadow lay curled up at the foot of her bed sound asleep – unmoved by her momentary panic.

Mary lay down again. She took a deep breath and her heart rate began to slow down. 'It must have been a dream', she told herself. She was unable to get back to sleep. She went to the bathroom and drank a glass of water. She put on a relaxation tape. She tried to read. Nothing seemed to help. Eventually she gave in and made her way downstairs and switched on the electric kettle.

The curtains across the patio windows were pulled back. Mary always opened them before she went to bed so that she could enjoy the view when she came down each morning. It was pitch black outside and the light from inside cast a dim glow over the grey patio paving stones. As she looked out she gasped as she was aware of a movement in the shadows beyond the light. Someone was out there. Instinctively she switched off the interior light and stared into the darkness.

Her heart was hammering in her chest – it must be Terry – he had tracked her down. He was outside the door. He had been looking in on her. Her legs gave way and she sank to the floor, her eyes never moving from the darkness beyond the large patio doors. She heard a footstep on the paving and then a crash as a flower pot was knocked over. Her mouth opened in a scream but no sound came out.

He could not get in. The security locks were the best money could buy. She must not panic. Where was the phone? She could not move. Her body felt paralysed but her mind was sharp and clear. The phone, she remembered, was on the kitchen dresser – she was sure that that was where she had last seen it. She would ring Howard as soon as she had recovered. He would not mind – he had said that she could ring him at any time.

It seemed like a long time afterwards but it was probably only a minute when she heard another sound from outside. There was a quiet tap on the glass and a small voice said, "Mary, Mary, are you there? It's Tom, Mary. Please let me in."

Mary's limbs were working again and she threw herself at the doors – unfastening the bolts as quickly as she could. In a matter of seconds Tom was in her arms sobbing uncontrollably, saying her name over and over again.

After about thirty minutes Tom's body began to relax – worn out by the efforts of crying. As he began to quieten, his voice changed. The desperation had changed to a more plaintive plea of, "Don't make me go back – don't let them take me back. Oh, Mary don't send me back there!"

Mary's face was full of compassion and utter hopelessness. She said nothing, just gently held him and stroked his wet hair. As he became more relaxed she managed to remove his wet coat and shoes and socks and she wrapped a warm rug, from the back of the couch, around him. Slowly the comfort of the place and the relief at having reached his goal allowed Tom to fall into a deep sleep.

Mary gazed at the sleeping child for quite a while – knowing that for the moment, at least, he had escaped from whatever torture he had been living in and, for the time being, he was safe from the demons which had tormented him.

How Mary remembered the wondrous arms of sleep. Sleep, for her, had been the most enormous safety net and comfort blanket at times like these. She was tempted to curl up next to the small figure and escape with him but she knew that she had some hard decisions to make and it was best that she make them while Tom was sleeping.

Mary was fully aware of the dangerous position Tom had unknowingly placed her in. She had once taken a child who was not her own and kept him hidden in her home. She could have gone to prison for that offense had her mind not given way. Now, here she was again, in a not dissimilar situation.

This was not quite the same but she could well imagine what the authorities would make of it – and even worse – what the press would make of it! What a story they would write. Her imagination ran wild and she felt a feeling of panic engulfing her. She knew that she could not handle this on her own. She would have to ring Howard even though it was the early hours of the morning.

Howard wakened and sat up in bed. It was very dark and he was surprised – he did not usually waken during the night. Something must have disturbed him – yes, there was a sound – a faint ringing in the distance. It took a moment or two before he realised that it was his mobile phone – it was still in his briefcase in the hall where he had dropped it the previous evening. He rushed down the stairs and grabbed the case – its insistent ringing even more demanding and urgent because of the lateness of the hour. Calls in the night were always bad news – some sort of crisis – this had always been the case, in his experience. He knew it was going to be Mary before he heard her voice.

"Oh, Thank Goodness!" she said, when he finally answered. "I'm so sorry to ring you at this hour, but it's an emergency. I need you to come here right away, Howard. Can you do that. I hate to ask, but there's no one else!"

"Yes, I'll come. I should be with you in about half an hour. There'll be no traffic at this time of night. You are on the main street, aren't you?"

"Yes, opposite the church – on your left. The lights will be on. Don't ring the bell – I'll be looking out for you. Please hurry!"

She had given no indication as to what manner of emergency this was but Howard was sure that it must be to do with her ex husband. He must have tracked her down somehow.

Howard was dressed and on his way within minutes. By the time he drew his car into the kerb at a house with its outside lights on, opposite the church, he was imagining all sorts of dramas being acted out there.

Mary was standing by the opened front door. She had slipped into a loose track suit while she awaited the arrival of her friend, the solicitor. She held her finger to her lips, then whispered, "Come through to the kitchen and I'll explain."

As Howard followed her through the half lit lounge he was surprised to see the figure of a small child fast asleep and covered by a fluffy blanket on the couch with a sleek grey cat curled up beside him.

Mary pulled the door closed behind them and gestured for him to sit down at the table. She had a pot of coffee ready and two blue and white mugs and sugar and milk laid neatly on the table. He could have been calling for morning coffee – it all looked so normal. Where, he wondered, was the emergency.

Mary still spoke in hushed tones, "I'm so sorry to drag you out like this but I am desperate."

"Is it to do with Terry?" Howard asked.

"Heavens, no," she exclaimed. "Whatever gave you that idea! It's Tom..." She gestured to the door into the lounge. "He's run away from school. He just turned up here about a couple of hours ago. I managed to get him calmed down and he fell fast asleep."

"Have you telephoned the school or the police then?" Howard asked.

"No, not yet. I'm in rather a delicate position you realise, with my history."

Howard looked perplexed.

"Remember I've been charged with child abduction in the past – when I took that baby!" she explained.

Howard began to grasp the seriousness of the situation and understood how his presence here, was indeed, a very wise precaution. This did need very careful handling.

"Do you think the school will know that the child has gone and will have alerted the authorities?"

"I don't know but it is possible that they may not have discovered he is missing and we have a few hours in which to plan what to do. He was hysterical when he got here and all he said was, 'Don't send me back – don't tell them I'm here.' and stuff like that. It's going to break my heart to let him down – but I've no alternative, have I?"

"No, you don't. It is vital that we handle this by the book. We need to avoid any publicity at all costs. The school will not want any either – so if we can speak to them before they call in the police so much the better. The parents are out of the country?.... Who do you think is in loco parentis, so to speak?"

"Probably the grandmother or aunt and uncle. I don't know any of them!"

"Right!" Howard looked at his watch. It was ten minutes past five. "I think it might be best if I ring the school on your behalf. Keep you right in the background. I'll tell the school what has happened and that Tom is perfectly safe here until the morning. I think we should arrange for the local doctor to examine him and assess the situation. Perhaps he could recommend that Tom remains here for a few days rest and recuperation. He would be able to speak to the school and the family from a professional stand point. It is preferable that you are involved as little as possible. It would really be best if they came and took the boy straight back to school – best for you that is but I can tell that you would not be happy for that to happen."

"I feel that I am letting him down already. He begged and begged me not to send him back. You should have heard him. Someone has got to listen to this child and find out what has driven him to this course of action. I know he will speak to me if we are given the chance. Getting a doctor involved is an excellent idea. I'll call my own doctor – Dr. Jacobs. I'm sure he was Tom's family doctor too. He is a lovely man – he knows how to listen. He'll put Tom first, I know he will. He knows all about me too, so that's a help."

"Right. Do you have the number for the school? I had better ring now just in case they are already aware that Tom has gone and have involved the police, family etc. Fingers crossed that this is the first they know of their pupil's disappearance."

Mary held her breath as Howard waited for someone to answer his call. The longer it took the more hopeful she became.

Howard too was tense. He knew that it would be so important that he handled this just right. He was certain that the school would want this incident dealt with, with as little fuss as possible – such an occurrence would do their reputation no good.

At last a rather sleepy, disembodied voice reached his ear, "Avonbury Hall. Can I help you?"

"Could I speak to the headmaster? It is a matter of some urgency." Howard said.

"I'll put you through. Hold the line for a moment." Yet another wait. It was clear that the school was asleep – no drama was as yet unfolding. Tom's departure was undiscovered and unreported. Howard put his thumb up to Mary and gave her a half smile.

"MacIntosh, here. How can I help you? Who's speaking?"

Howard swallowed and began to explain who he was and why he was ringing. He put the facts very simply – glossing over Mary's involvement – saying merely that she lived next door to Tom's former home. It was all very matter of fact and undramatic. Howard said that Tom was fast asleep and perfectly safe and that the doctor would check him over when he awoke. Howard said that he would arrange for the doctor to ring the school and the family after he had examined Tom if Mr. MacIntosh agreed that this was the best way to proceed. Howard did say that Tom had been in an extremely distraught state when he turned up and that he did need gentle handling and that, in his opinion, rushing him straight back to school might not be in the child's best interest.

The headmaster obviously needed time to think about all of this and was glad to go along with Howard's suggestions in the meantime. He said that he would inform the family as soon as it was morning. There was no need to ring them right away, under the circumstances. No need for any panic now that he knew that Tom was safe and well. He thanked Howard for getting in touch so promptly.

Mary sat stunned – she felt dead inside. She knew that she was betraying Tom in order to save her own skin. She was not proud of what she was doing. She felt sick and full of disgust at herself. She had gone back years to that feeling of self loathing. She had never imagined experiencing this ever again. Her face was grey and her eyes had sunk back into her skull.

Howard was shocked when he turned from the phone and looked at Mary. She looked like a stranger. For the first time he was able to catch a glimpse of the young woman he remembered in his boss's office with her father, all these years ago. He was afraid that this turn of events had pushed her over the edge and back into the abyss.

Had this been brought about by the reappearance of her ex husband he would not have been too surprised. This too, he was aware, was connected to her dark past ! If she had not been in trouble with the police all these years ago when she abducted that baby she would not have been so compromised now. She would not have been forced to go against her natural instincts, which were to protect this child at all costs – at whatever cost to herself.

Howard moved towards Mary and put his hand on hers – it was icy cold. "It's all right, Mary. We'll sort it out somehow. You had no choice. Take a deep breath – come on, you can do it. You need to gather yourself before Tom wakes up."

This last comment seemed to reach her and she moved at last

and, to Howard's relief, she proceeded to go into her recovery routine. It took longer than it had taken when she had used the technique in his office but eventually she stretched her arms to the ceiling and beyond and managed to smile.

"Thank you, Howard. I'd lost it for a while there. I was back in that pit – that black place. I didn't think I could come back. If you hadn't been here..........." She paused, imagining the unimaginable.

"You're doing really well, Mary. Just stay focused. Now that we have done what had to be done we can concentrate on how best to help Tom."

"You're right, Howard. Absolutely right. I need to be strong for him. I'm going to do everything I can to make it up to him. He's going to hate me for doing this. I wish that I could explain to him why I had to betray him in this way. Maybe some day he will understand."

FIFTEEN

Tom stirred and opened his eyes. Where was he? He saw the grey cat snuggled into his side and knew where he was. Everything was all right. He was at Mary's. She wouldn't let him down. She would not let them take him back to that hateful place. He would stay here with her and Shadow and go to his old school again until his parents returned from Borneo. It was all going to work out just fine.

His attention was drawn to the kitchen door. A desperate, sick feeling clawed at his stomach. He could hear voices – soft whispering voices coming from the kitchen. He could recognise Mary's voice and a man's voice. 'Oh no!' he thought. 'She has told someone – was it the headmaster come to drag him back or was it perhaps the police?' He moved over to the door and put his ear close to the wood panelling. He had to know what they were saying. He could not make out the words properly but the man was speaking very gently to Mary. He sounded kind and caring. Instinctively Tom knew that this was someone who knew Mary quite well – this was no stranger, no first meeting. So it could not be the police or someone from school. Mary must have a friend or relative staying. He began to relax a little though there was a bit inside him that did not feel too comfortable about Mary having someone else in her life.

He heard the scraping sound of a chair moving on the tiled floor and he hurried back to the couch not wanting to be caught listening by the door. He lay still, pulling the blanket up to his chin. He heard the door being opened carefully and almost noiselessly, then Mary tiptoed over and looked down on him. He opened his eyes and smiled, "Hi, Mary. I've had such a good sleep."

Mary looked at the small figure. She saw the curve of his body beneath the blanket, his dark tousled hair and, to her dismay, the deep trusting look in his big brown eyes. She looked away, ashamed. She could not meet those eyes. How could she tell him what she had done?

"Tom" she said, "I'm sorry, but I had to let the school know that you were here. They.........." She got no further. Tom sat up, pushing aside the protective cover and getting to his feet, looking towards the door, seeking his escape route. "How could you, Mary?" he screamed. "I told you. I told you I could never go back. I trusted you! I hate you! I hate you!"

She turned away – each word hit her like a knife cutting into her flesh or a boot kicking into her sides. She hugged her arms around her chest – instinctively protecting herself.

Howard had moved into the room and gently approached the enraged child. "Tom, Tom" he said, reaching out to quiet the flying limbs. "It's all right, Tom. It's all right!" Tom seemed to recognise his kindness and, though he was a stranger, he seemed to melt into his arms, exhausted by this further emotional outburst. He dissolved into desperate sobbing – his small body racked and rocking with inner pain and torment. The tall man had dropped to his knees and the two heads were side by side facing opposite directions.

Mary watched transfixed as if watching a scene in a play – an outsider looking in. Her eyes met Howards – his lips were moving – he was speaking to her, mouthing the words...... 'Ring the doctor – go on. Do it now' It seemed to take forever but eventually the message reached her brain and her paralysed body began to respond. She moved towards the kitchen and her phone. As she left the room she began to take control again.

She dialed the number, glancing at the clock on the wall as she did so. It was seven seventeen. On the third ring the warm reassuring voice of Dr. Jacobs answered. Quickly and concisely Mary told him what had occurred and what she wanted him to do. He understood at once and promised he would be with her in less than half an hour.

She re-entered the room and nodded to Howard who was still holding and rocking the small boy in his arms. From somewhere deep within her came a feeling of longing to be held like that, by this man. In that moment her whole being was crying out to be hugged close – to escape the pain and the fear in such an embrace. She had had need of this for all of her life.

Mary moved quietly into the hallway and took up a position beside the front door – holding it open awaiting the arrival of the doctor. The minutes dragged by but eventually a silver coloured car slowed to a stop on the edge of the footpath and the balding head of Dr. Jacobs emerged. He reached into the interior of the car and pulled out his battered medical bag and hurried towards her.

"He's in the sitting room with Howard – my solicitor." Mary said as she lead the way across the small hallway.

Dr. Peter Jacobs was a man of average height in his late fifties. He had lost his hair at an early age but had the handsome good looks that many balding men exhibit. There is an openness to their face which seems to accentuate the eyes – no hair to distract or indeed to hide behind. He had an air of authority and quiet confidence. When he entered a room he somehow was in charge – people seemed to step back and let him have centre stage. This just happened and was always a matter of some surprise to the unassuming doctor.

He moved quietly and unhurriedly into Mary's dimly lit sitting room. Howard was relieved to see the doctor's arrival. He said gently, "Tom, the doctor is here to see you," and he moved the exhausted little body back onto the couch, easing him carefully from his arms.

Tom looked up fearfully – scared of more intrusion, more authority. He was somewhat relieved to see the familiar face of a man he had known all of his life, someone who had always been kind, someone who had always listened to what he had to say.

"Oh, Doctor Peter," he said, as he lay back into the cushions, his face red and swollen – blotchy and tear stained.

"It's all right, Tom. You've had a bad time. I can see that. I'm here to help you."

"Don't let them send me back. Please, please, don't let them." His voice began to crack again. He was becoming hysterical again.

The doctor had taken his wrist and was taking his pulse – concentrating on his watch as he did so. This seemed to steady Tom.

His voice took on a quiet calmness and he said, "If you send me back I will kill myself!" The impact of these words was unimaginable. The three adults felt the full force of these words. This was no hysterical outburst – no manipulative empty threat. This was a quiet statement of intent – an honest factual prediction and they each knew that Tom meant every word of it.

They were fully aware of the possible horror of what the child had said and they feared for him. They appreciated, in that moment, that whatever had happened to Tom at school was a greater fear for him than death itself!

It seemed an eternity until anyone spoke – Tom's words hung in the air like a huge cloud of poisonous gas.

The doctor let go of Tom's wrist and said, "O.K, Tom. I'll tell you what we are going to do. I'm going to give you something to help you to calm down and relax a bit. Then I want you to go to the kitchen with Mary and have a drink and some toast or cereal while I ring your school and grandmother and arrange that you stay here for a while, until you feel better.

At this, Tom burst in, "She doesn't want me here – she wants to send me back. I hate her!"

He looked in fury at Mary.

"Oh, I don't, Tom. I really don't!" Mary's tone was begging him to believe her.

"Tom, Tom, listen to me." It was the doctor's authoritative voice again. "Mary had to call the school. She had no choice. She would have been in very serious trouble indeed if she had not. Mary did not want to do it. Do you understand? She would have been in trouble with the police if she had kept you here."

Tom heard what the doctor was saying and he understood and looked into Mary's eyes and saw her look of love and compassion and he reached out to her.

She held him as the doctor gave him a shot of light sedative.

"Let's do what the doctor said, Tom. Have some breakfast and then you can go upstairs to bed. Shadow, I expect, will keep you company. Could you manage a boiled egg, do you think?"

The tall slim woman and the small dishevelled boy in a crumpled school uniform made their way towards the kitchen hand in hand and the grey cat followed them. It seemed to Howard as if a degree of harmony had returned after a long period of discord – a beautiful friendship re- established. It was, he thought, as if a plate had broken in two and now its jagged torn edges had been neatly matched back together – almost a perfect repair but not quite. Mary had, he felt, slipped slightly from the pedestal on which Tom had placed her and this, Howard knew, was a good thing. Friendship, in his opinion, worked best if an eye to eye level was maintained – looking up or even down would eventually lead to strain and friction and disharmony.

The two men – the lawyer and the doctor, faced one another – the telephone on the table between them. There was a mutual respect one for the other and an awareness of the extreme delicacy of the situation they were both faced with. Both men were battling with their different areas of professionalism and their instincts of what was best for the child in the midst of this mayhem.

Both men realised fully that allowing Tom to remain in the care of a known child abductor, with a long history of severe mental illness, was a decision that would be more than frowned on by their respective professional bodies and by the authorities. But they both knew, that for the immediate future, this was the best place for Tom to remain. He needed stability and peace and he had chosen Mary – this was the only place the boy felt safe. These were familiar surroundings with good memories – a place where he could find the security he so desperately required.

The two men silently mulled over the possible options available to them.

"I could have the boy admitted to a children's psychiatric ward," the doctor said, his tone and expression disregarding his own suggestion as he said it.

"It's a bugger......." Howard responded, feeling sympathy for the doctor who ultimately had the decision to make.

"I can't do it. I'm going to recommend he remains here for a couple of days with Mary and under my medical care! What do you think?"

"I agree, but if it ever comes out about Mary's past, we'll both be in big trouble. However, I have to agree, that if we are thinking of what is in Tom's best interest, you are quite right. This is the best place for him right now. I'll be here as much as I can, if that would help?"

The doctor had made up his mind and he reached for the telephone reading the numbers from the card which Mary had left beside the phone.

The doctor spoke with an assurance and certainty that he had not shown a few minutes before and it was apparent to Howard that the headmaster, at the other end of the telephone, was listening intently to this professional man. Dr. Jacobs explained in detail his medical opinion on the young runaway's physical, mental and emotional state and gave his recommendations for his immediate care. The doctor did not underestimate the seriousness of Tom's condition and the importance of the decisions to be made. He stressed that taking him back to school at this time would be disastrous and that he felt that immediate hospitalisation too, might be equally traumatic and dangerous.

There was a silence in the room as the voice on the other end spoke at some length. Howard strained to hear and stared at the doctor's face trying to analyse his facial expression and body language. The doctor gazed at the far wall as if absorbed in the wallpaper design. Then he said, "Yes, I understand. Perhaps I should speak to them. Give me the numbers." As he spoke, he reached for the pen on the far side of the coffee table and began to write. "Shall I get back to you when I have spoken to the family?.... Very well." He switched off the mobile phone and placed it on the table.

"Well...?" inquired the impatient solicitor.

"So far, so good. The school seems happy to go along with my suggestions but the family have the ultimate decision. I shall ring them now. First the grandmother and then, I expect, the parents in Borneo."

He lifted the phone again. This time it was apparent that he was speaking to someone more emotionally charged – someone who wanted to know everything but could not stop asking questions and making suggestions. The doctor was struggling, as soon as he spoke he was interrupted. After trying to speak a few times he stopped and became silent – holding the telephone away from his ear. His eyes met Howards in exasperation. After a minute or two the voice at the other end stopped. Howard heard a woman's voice say loudly, "Are you still there, Doctor?"

"Yes, I am here, Mrs. Pearson. I understand how upset you are but I really need you to listen – don't say anything until I finish. Can you do that for me?" This might have sounded patronising but somehow it came over as caring, yet authoritative and, to Howard's amazement, Mrs. Pearson went quiet.

With the most remarkable powers of patience and persuasion the doctor seemed to succeed in reassuring Tom's grandmother that Tom was in the best place with the best possible care and that her supportive appearance on the scene was not necessary or advisable at the moment and that the good doctor himself would keep in close contact with her and advise her when the time was right for her to visit her grandson. Right now Tom needed absolute quiet and complete rest.

When the doctor at last laid down the phone onto the table top he collapsed back into the chair with a huge explosion of breath from pursed lips and grinned at the lawyer opposite as if he was a fellow conspirator.

"Right, now for the parents. What time do you think it will be in Borneo?"

"If my memory serves me right it should be around tea time there." Howard replied with some confidence. He was glad to have been able to contribute something of use to the proceedings.

Peter Jacobs straightened up, took a deep breath and started to feed the vast list of numbers into the phone. His face was serious. He knew Tom's parents and was feeling less than happy about the forthcoming conversation.

The call was answered and he asked to speak to either Mr. or Mrs. Livingstone. After a few moments he was trying to explain to Mr. Livingstone why he was ringing – hurriedly reassuring him that there was nothing to worry about, that Tom was safe and that he had agreed to ring rather than the headmaster so that he could give him a full medical report on his son, following his ordeal.

Howard admired the doctor's clear and succinct appraisal of the situation. It became evident, after a few minutes, that the doctor did not like the stance that Mr. Livingstone was adopting. The doctor's tone altered. He became more forceful and authoritative.

"This, I can assure you, Mr. Livingstone, is not merely a childish prank – neither is it an act of defiance on the part of your son. He is, as I said, mentally and emotionally exhausted and I cannot emphasize enough how crucial it is that this situation is handled with the utmost delicacy and care. Mishandling, at this stage, could be very serious indeed."

It was obvious to Howard that the doctor did not like the man at the other end of the phone and he had to admire the tact and diplomacy and control of the man opposite as he put the case of his young patient.

"No, there is absolutely no need for you or your wife to fly home immediately. Take time, think about all that I have said and then ring me at home later." He gave the number slowly and deliberately. "Ring tomorrow at this time and I will be able to tell you more. I will also be in touch with the school and your wife's mother. Yes, if that is what you wish – I will arrange for a consultant pediatrician to come out and examine your son and you can have a second opinion from him."

The call finished quite abruptly and the doctor leant back, raised his hands to the ceiling and shrugged his shoulders in exasperation. "What an arrogant bastard...... Excuse my French. Poor Tom.... Thank goodness the parents are out of the country. Let's hope they stay put for a while!"

He looked at his watch and gasped, "I'll have to fly – morning surgery! Will you be around for a while? I will come back around twelve to have another look at Tom."

Howard said that he could stay until the afternoon but he had to be back in his office by two.

"Right we will meet here at twelve and have a chat about everything then."

The doctor hurried into the kitchen to have a word with Mary then was hurrying towards the front door.

A few minutes later Tom and Mary appeared from the kitchen still hand in hand. They walked towards Howard. "This is my good friend, Howard, Tom. I know you have already met but let's do it officially. Howard, this is Tom, a very special friend of mine."

The small boy and the tall man shook hands.

"Tom is going to go upstairs now to have a nice long rest. Dr. Jacobs said he has to have lots of sleep and he is coming back to check on him around lunch time. Come on, Tom. You can go into the little bedroom at the back. It is nice and quiet."

When Mary reappeared she looked strained and exhausted. She collapsed down onto the couch beside Howard. "You've been great, Howard. I don't know how I would have coped without you. Thank you!"

"I'm glad you had the sense to ring me. Your doctor is a marvellous fellow – one in a million, I should say. I told him that I would wait here until he gets back, if that's all right with you?"

Mary's eyes filled with tears, "Are you sure? You've done more than enough already."

Mary went to make more coffee and Howard rang his office.

Tom fell fast asleep in Mary's spare bedroom and the grey cat curled up beside him at the foot of the light blue, checkered duvet.

SIXTEEN

It was twelve fifteen later that same day when Mary opened the door to Dr. Jacobs again. She had prepared more coffee and a large plate of sandwiches and, after she had checked that the child upstairs was still sound asleep, the three adults settled around the kitchen table.

The doctor had little more to report but he was able to tell the other two exactly what had been said during his earlier telephone calls.

The school had been only too happy to allow the doctor to take charge on the understanding that they were kept closely informed. Tom's grandmother had needed some persuasion to prevent her from racing down to see Tom. The doctor had been able to stall her temporarily but he was doubtful as to how long he could keep her away. This was quite understandable.

As for Tom's father, he had been the most difficult. Mary was not at all surprised at the tone he had adopted when he heard what had happened to his son. She had never taken to the man and knew that Tom was afraid of him. If he had had his way Tom would already have been returned to his rightful place back at school with an accompanying clip around his ear.

The three became very quiet when she expressed this opinion. They were all remembering what Tom had said earlier – each of them knew the seriousness of the situation and feared that they might be powerless to prevent an unspeakable tragedy.

"I have spoken to the Pediatric Consultant from The General about Tom and he has agreed to come and examine him this evening, as a favour to me." Doctor Jacobs continued. "I told him it was specially urgent because of the parents being out of the country and that they were ringing me in the morning for further news. I shall bring him round between seven and eight tonight. Is that all right, Mary?"

She nodded. Her head was in turmoil. She was so full of fear for Tom and she felt impotent – she could only do what she was allowed to do to help him and she had a gripping dread that some invisible hand was about to drop down and snatch him away from her. It was almost unbearable. The two fine men seated opposite were equally helpless but she felt grateful that they understood and cared about the young boy upstairs.

When Howard and the doctor left for the afternoon, Mary went upstairs and sat quietly in the rocking chair in the corner of Tom's room. She wanted to be close by when he woke up. She wanted him to feel safe and loved. She began to relax. Her eyes closed and she slept.

Mary awoke with a start and found Tom standing beside her touching her knee. He looked lost and bewildered and she pulled him into her arms and held him. She felt his arms tighten around her and it was as if he never wanted to let her go.

"You won't let them send me back, will you, Mary?"

"I'll do all I can, Tom. So will Doctor Peter – but it won't be up to us, I'm afraid. I wish that I could give you a promise. But I can't. If it was up to me you could stay here. You know that!"

"I won't go back. I won't!" He said

"Was it so awful, Tom?"

He began to cry again and in a voice racked with sobs he began to tell her. "They were so mean to me, Mary. I didn't do anything to them. They just picked on me all the time. They called me names. They found my special moment oil that you gave me and they laughed at me – they called me a poofter for wearing perfume. They tore up your letters – the ones with the lovely drawings and they kept on calling me names....... I tried to be brave and ignore them but I couldn't. ..... They said that they would beat me up if I told anyone........ It was just awful........ I couldn't stand it any more .... I just had to get away and I won't ever go back......Not ever........ I would rather be dead......"

Tears were running down Mary's cheeks and she was filled with anger. Had these bullies been in front of her she would have killed them, she felt sure.

"Oh, Tom...... Oh, Tom..." was all she could say. She rocked him in her arms.

SEVENTEEN

Howard Hamilton had a passion for classic cars. This was his hobby as well as his means of transport. His car, at present, and the immediate love of his life, was a nineteen fifty eight, MGB, G.T. in mint condition in a glorious shade of yellow. Only other car enthusiasts can understand the depth of feelings a man can have for such a machine.

This bright yellow car was well known in the community – it was hard to miss. People in the surrounding area knew exactly where the good looking solicitor spent his time – be it at the golf course – at the pub – or out walking on the moors. Wherever his car was parked, someone who knew him seemed to see it.

That Friday evening, as Howard left his office and headed once again towards Ashtonbury to give Mary his ongoing support, the bright yellow car was, as usual, observed and recognised.

Terry Harrison had been feeling extremely frustrated at his lack of progress in finding Rachel. He was ninety nine per cent sure that the Mary Parker he had located in the files in Howard Hamilton's office, and Rachel, were one and the same person. The dates fitted – the connection with Rachel's father's solicitor was there – and most damning of all, the absence of an address on the file, was extremely suspicious. Mary Parker was certainly a woman who did not want to be found.

Terry had hoped to pick up Rachel's trail at the Post Office collection point but had been thwarted here by the discovery that Howard Hamilton appeared to collect the mail on Mary's behalf. The solicitor, therefore, must know the exact whereabouts of his mysterious client.

At every opportunity, after this discovery, Terry had watched the comings and goings of the yellow sports car and its occupant. He had learned a lot about the life of the car owner but nothing at all about that of his client.

That weekend Terry had decided to give himself a break. He was feeling downhearted and frustrated. He was heading home after a particularly rotten day and was planning a night in a pub somewhere, maybe some female company and a chance to relax and have some fun for a change.

He was anticipating this as he drove along, the music on his stereo playing loudly to get him in the mood. Suddenly a yellow sports car caught his eye, travelling in the opposite direction. 'Where's he off to?' he wondered and as soon as he could he turned around and set off in pursuit of the yellow sports car.

It was a few miles before he saw the tail lights of the yellow car up ahead. He had been beginning to think that he had lost him. He kept well back. Terry was feeling sort of excited inside. He knew that this was the journey that he had been waiting for the solicitor to make. He did not believe in coincidences. For some reason he had a certainty that the man he was following was on his way to see Mary Parker!

The yellow car was slowing down. It stopped beside a row of houses opposite a church. The occupant of the car got out and went to a door and rang the bell and was admitted after a few moments. Terry could not make out the figure who opened the door.

The house, when he looked at it, had a strange appearance. What was it that made it so peculiar? He suddenly realised – it had no windows onto the street – only the blue door set into a grey stone wall. He felt more certain than ever that this was the house where his ex wife was hiding out.

Terry sat in the car. He was feeling good but he wanted to be sure. Just then he noticed the door of the darkened church open and a short elderly woman, carrying a basket coming out. He moved rapidly. He slipped out of his car and walked towards the church gates.

"Excuse me" he said, "sorry to bother you, but I am looking for a relative of mine and I am not sure which house she lives in. It's around here somewhere. She's called Mary Parker."

"Oh, yes. I know who you mean. Tall lady, lives alone – been in the village about two to three years? She lives right across there at Orchard Cottage." She raised her arm and pointed to the house with the yellow sports car at the door.

Just then a second car stopped and two men got out – each carrying a small case.

"Oh, that's Dr. Jacobs. Mrs. Parker must be ill. Oh dear, I hope it's nothing serious." The lady looked concerned.

Thanks for your help," Terry said, holding the gate to the churchyard open to let her pass.

"That's all right. I hope everything's all right!"

Terry watched the woman until she disappeared at the end of the street then he made his way back to his car smiling to himself. "Gotcha!" He whispered under his breath. So this was where Rachel was hiding herself away – obviously she had not begun to spend her inheritance yet. This was a small insignificant dwelling place. She could have afforded much better than this.

She must still be ill with the doctor calling at this time of night. He hoped the shock of receiving his card had not sent her over the edge again. He was concerned that the arrival of two doctors and her solicitor might indicate that his ex wife was about to become sectioned again and admitted to hospital. This would not suit him at all. He did not want to have to fight his way past medical staff in order to see her. He wanted her vulnerable, lonely and needy.

Terry was also a little anxious about that solicitor in the flashy sports car – he hoped this association was nothing other than professional. She was a good catch and as far as he could gather, Howard Hamilton seemed to be single.

They were taking their time, he thought. She must be paying for this much attention – no one got this sort of service on the National Health these days.

Inside the house there was indeed much discussion taking place. The two doctors had spoken with Mary at great length then spent some time upstairs with Tom.

The boy was now asleep again having had another sedative from the doctor. Tom had become quite hysterical when questioned, about why he had run away from school, by the kindly pediatrician.

The three men and Mary sat drinking coffee – all solemn faced and concerned.

"If we could make the decisions without interference from the parents on this one, I would not be too concerned," said the consultant. "Tom can easily and quickly recover from this episode if he is allowed to quit the boarding school and be in a loving and stable environment. He needs rest and some counselling to make sure he does not blame himself for anything that has happened."

"This is the best scenario," said Dr. Jacobs. "However, if his parents refuse to accept this and insist that he go back to school…. Well, this child, in my opinion, will break completely – and I am not scaremongering. Do you not agree?" he asked his colleague.

The consultant nodded in agreement, "We must be prepared that this might happen."

"Could we then have Tom made a ward of court?" Howard suggested.

"Yes, as a last resort, I would be prepared to advocate this." said the consultant grimly. "Naturally, I hope this can be avoided. We will have a better idea tomorrow after we have spoken to the parents again. We will both put Tom's case as strongly as we possibly can."

Doctor Jacobs turned to Mary and said, "He should be feeling more lively tomorrow after another night's sleep. You can cope with him for another day or so, can you? It is best not to move him yet. He needs the stability. I may have to allow a visit from his grandmother tomorrow. Are you comfortable with that? She may be a little awkward with you – put out that he chose to run to a stranger rather than to her!"

"I'll handle it." Mary said quietly.

"I can be here with you, if you want?" Howard volunteered.

"That would be an excellent idea." Dr. Jacobs answered before Mary could express an opinion.

Mary was unaware of what was going on in the minds of her

doctor and her solicitor – they were watching their backs!

The two medical men got up to leave. It was Howard who accompanied them to the door. He went back inside to have a few words with Mary before he let himself out of the front door and made his way towards his car. He was unaware that someone was following his every move as he climbed inside and started the engine.

Terry silently watched these departures from the dark safety of his car. There was no more for him to do that night. He would return to keep watch again next morning. He would bide his time. He had to be sure. He had to plan his next move with the utmost care.

Tom slept peacefully – the light sedative ensuring a night free from restlessness and panicky distress and relived nightmares.

Mary slept less deeply – she was alert to any sound from the child tucked up in the bed in the room next door. She had to work hard to keep her mind from dwelling on dark imaginings and unbearable, frightening outcomes of the unfolding drama.

The grey cat was on guard duty – watching over the small boy who had protected her when threatened, as a kitten, with a watery grave. She slept peacefully on the small boy's bed – a comforting area of warmth beside Tom's legs.

As predicted, Tom seemed more like himself the following morning and he pottered around in the kitchen helping Mary prepare breakfast. He fed the cat. He was wearing an old tartan dressing gown of Mary's. It reached almost to the floor. He had not wanted to wear his school clothes since he took them off before climbing into the bed in Mary's upstairs room, such a short time ago.

It was around ten thirty when Howard returned. This time he was weighed down by an armful of carrier bags. He had brought provisions for Mary and had also bought some clothes for Tom – underwear, pyjamas and a navy and red track suit.

Mary was impressed – this man never ceased to amaze her.

"You go upstairs now, Tom, and you can put on these new clothes."

Tom did as he was told and left the room clutching the bags. "Thank you, Howard," he said as he left the two adults.

"He seems much brighter this morning. Did he have a good night? And how about you?" Howard asked, watching her closely.

"I'm fine and yes, Tom is much better. I'm a bit concerned though that anyone seeing him like this will think that there is nothing wrong with him and decide to bundle him off, back to school."

"Have you heard anything yet from Peter?" Howard asked.

"He rang this morning, after his phone call with Tom's parents. He said that he'll be round later and Tom's grandmother will be visiting Tom today. I think Tom may go back with her." Mary's voice was sad and full of concern.

"Well that might be for the best. We don't want him getting too comfortable here – because that can never be a long term solution." Howard sounded like the legal advisor.

"Yes, I know that," Mary said, sounding slightly irritated, "but I am worried about Tom. "I have told him that his grandmother is coming and he did not seem to mind. I think he likes her, so that is a relief. I will feel better when I have met her I expect."

When the doctor arrived he was pleased to see the improvement in his patient. Mary sent Tom out into the garden with Shadow so that they could talk privately.

"Well," the doctor began. "The good news is that Tom's father can't come home right now – pressure of work. Tom's mother is on her way home as soon as she can arrange a flight and they want Tom to go and stay with his grandmother in York in the meantime. I think this is the best we could hope for. They have agreed to leave Tom's medical care in the hands of John Fellows – they obviously took a liking to him when they spoke to him on the telephone and he will liaise with the local G.P."

The doctor turned to Howard, a look of concern on his face, "Did you, by any chance happen to notice a dark blue escort parked across the street when you arrived? It was there last night as well and I am sure there was a man sitting in it both times. I hope the press have not got wind of what's been happening here."

"Oh no!" Howard said, his eyes looking straight into Mary's. A look of horror passed between the two of them. "That damned yellow car of mine. I may as well have laid a paint trail to your door, Mary. Oh, I am so sorry. How could I have been so stupid...... It must be Terry!"

The doctor was looking mystified. He hadn't a clue as to what was going on between Mary and Howard but he was aware of their distress. "What are you on about?" he asked.

Howard answered and quickly gave him a synopsis of what had happened – the newspaper articles, the break in, the birthday card etc.

"Right," said the doctor. "It is even more important than ever that Tom leaves today and it would be best if whoever is watching does not see him go. We do not want any complications at this stage."

"First of all I want to make sure that it really is Terry out there," Howard said, getting to his feet. "I'll walk along to the shop and buy some milk." He was gone before either of the two said a word.

"I can't see how we are to get Tom away without being seen." Mary said. "We don't want the grandmother to know of our concern."

Both went quiet mulling over the problem, both hoping that Howard would return soon to tell them that there was no blue escort parked in the street outside and no Terry lurking in the shadows.

In no time at all Howard was back with the unnecessary carton of milk. He looked so miserable that he did not need to say anything. Mary spoke right away. "Please don't blame yourself, Howard. We are both to blame. We let our defenses down in our anxiety about Tom. It's unfortunate but it was really only a matter of time. At least we are forewarned and have time to plan how best to get Tom from the house without Terry seeing him. It would just suit Terry to have the press get their grubby little hands into all of this with Tom and have them rake up all of my past."

Several ideas were put forward but the best suggestion seemed to be the most obvious one. One of them would simply ring the local police and, acting as a kind of unofficial neighbourhood watch member, mention that they were concerned about a man in a blue escort acting suspiciously. Howard had memorised the car registration when he was out. They all felt sure that if Terry was approached by the police he would disappear for an hour or so and that would give Tom time to leave with his grandmother, unobserved.

They talked it through and decided that the police would act more promptly if the caller was a woman. Mary pulled a face but agreed to make the phone call.

EIGHTEEN

Terry had been watching the comings and goings from the house with the blue door. It was a tedious job, sitting and watching, hour after hour but he was encouraged by the thought that he had almost reached his goal. He sat and mused over how he would work his way back into Rachel's life and eventually take over the management of her vast fortune.

The doctor had been again. He must be worried about her or else he was just lining his pockets with extra, unnecessary, private house calls. He would soon put a stop to all of that kind of nonsense. There was no need for such needless expense. He would not allow people to take advantage in this way!

That lawyer fellow was hanging around a lot too – running out for milk – just like an odd job boy – hardly legal work. He had brought bags of shopping with him when he arrived that morning – a proper little home help. Another one on the make, he thought cynically.

Terry was just lighting up another cigarette when someone tapped on his car window making him jump. A policeman, in uniform, opened the car door and said, "Can I have a word with you, sir?"

"What's the problem, officer? I'm not on a double yellow line am I?"

"Nothing like that. I've just had a complaint about you from the local neighbourhood watch. They are concerned that you seem to be hanging around here rather a lot. You have been here over the last couple of days according to our caller. Do you mind giving me your name and address, sir. I'll take a look at your driving license, while I'm at it."

"Is all this really necessary, constable? I'm just putting in some time.

I've an appointment later and I had some time to kill......... Just thought this was a quiet street and I could rest up for a bit and have a smoke. No harm in that, surely? I'll get going, if that's all you want." Terry reached out for his keys.

"Yes, I think that's a very good idea." The policeman said. " But I'll take your details just the same – for my report, you understand."

Police involvement was the last thing Terry wanted and he did as he was asked and drove off. He would have to pull his head in for a while, a few days at least. He would have to make sure his car was not seen in this area for the foreseeable future.

Later, when the doctor left, there was no sign of the blue escort and all three drew a sigh of relief.

When the policeman rang Mary later, he reported that the car driver had been moved on, and that, in his opinion, there did not seem anything sinister about the man's presence outside her house. Mary thanked him and apologised for troubling him and agreed with him that it had probably been her overactive imagination. However she knew differently – she knew that Terry had found out where she lived and more than that, she knew that he would be back.

Tom seemed pleased to see his grandmother and Mary was reassured when she observed her gentleness with her grandson. She had obviously listened to the doctor's reports and did not mention anything which might upset Tom. Tom pulled her outside to be introduced to Shadow. Shadow was singularly unimpressed and hurried off into the bushes.

Tom's grandmother was probably in her middle fifties but dressed much younger. She wore a neat black suit – an uncharitable observer might have commented that the jacket was a little tight and the skirt a little short. She had a pleasant, open face, carefully made up and her hair was well cut and nicely coloured.

She appeared a little suspicious of Mary at first but thanked her for her kindness and concern for Tom and, when Tom asked if he would be allowed to ring Mary and perhaps visit again, she assured him that this would be possible. Tom brightened when he heard this and beamed at Mary.

When Tom disappeared upstairs to collect something, his grandmother confided in Mary, "I never approved of them sending the children away to school. It's probably fine for Cathy but I told them that it would never do for a sensitive child like Tom." Mary warmed to her. "If it had been left to my daughter he would never have gone. But my son-in-law, well...... I shouldn't say this, but he's a hard, arrogant man, who likes his own way – a bit of a bully, you might say!" She stopped talking as Tom reappeared carrying a drawing book and pencils.

"I'm ready now, Grandma," the small boy said. "I'll ring you, Mary, when we get to Grandma's." He went to Mary and hugged her and whispered, "I'm sorry I said that I hated you. I didn't mean it!"

Mary hugged him to her and said, "I'll always be here for you if you need me!" She meant it. Terry was not going to chase her away. She had to stand and fight.

Howard left soon after and Mary was on her own at last. She needed this space. Her ordered, quiet, controlled life had been turned upside down over these last few days. She could not believe that this time of turmoil had, in fact, been so short – it felt like weeks since she had had the house to herself.

Mary suddenly felt exhausted. She headed for the bath tub but could not find the energy even for that. She lay down on her bed and fell fast asleep. When she wakened it was dark and she thought that it must be the middle of the night. She heard the phone ringing and her heart began to pound. Who could be ringing at this time of night? She rushed down the stairs and seized the phone, "yes?" she said.

"Hi, Mary. It's me." Tom's voice sounded calm. She looked at her watch – it was six thirty. It was only early evening!

"Hello, Tom. How are you doing?"

"I'm fine. Grandma and me had a Macdonald's on the way to her house. I had a Big Mac and large fries and coke. Mummy rang and she'll be home the day after tomorrow. She didn't sound mad at me." He lowered his voice and whispered, "I'm glad Daddy wasn't there. I'm glad he's not coming!"

"I'm sure things will work out fine, Tom. I'm missing you and so is Shadow. We'll talk again soon."

She laid the phone down and laughed nervously as her feelings of panic began to fade. She had worked herself into a state but it was not really surprising.

The house seemed strangely quiet and empty. This was how it had always been – just the way she liked it – somehow it did not feel quite the same. She had moved on again – for the last few days she had been part of the outside world. It felt as if she had stepped out of prison for a few hours then been put back into her cell. This surprised her. She had had a taste of normal life – if you could call the dramatic turn of events normal – and she had, she realised, liked the interaction – the communication - the emotional exchanges and most of all, the companionship.

She was mulling this over when the phone rang again. She put it to her ear and heard Howard's voice. "Just rang to see how you are. It must be strange to have your house to yourself again."

"I'm fine. I slept for hours after you'd gone and then Tom rang. He sounded fine. I really think he will be if nobody rocks the boat. How about you? You must be glad to have your life back again?"

"Oh me, I'm fine but I have been giving this Terry issue some thought. I can't believe I was so stupid, so short sighted. I might as well have put a sign on your door – Mary Parker lives here! At least Terry can't imagine that we are on to him. He'd never imagine we'd be that stupid."

"Don't beat yourself up. Terry has been inching his way towards me and it is now only a matter of where and when we confront each other and I am beginning to think the sooner the better. All this with Tom has made me realise that I want to be back in the real world. I want my driving license and my passport. I want to stop looking over my shoulder. I want to stop hiding away like a criminal."

"That's so good to hear. I think this might be time to employ my private investigator. I have the make and number of Terry's car – he will find him easily. He will find out what he is up to – build up a dossier – maybe take a few photographs. Then, when you are ready to confront him, there will be no surprises and it can be on your terms."

Mary felt empowered by this suggestion and agreed to it straight away. She could take control. This was how it had to be. She smiled to herself imagining how surprised Terry was going to be. He had never known her in control, strong and confident and this was how she wanted him to see her.

Howard said that he would set it all up the following morning and that he would keep her posted.

Mary felt much better after this call and she made herself something to eat before settling down in front of the television to watch a movie. It was a predictable, unabsorbing sort of film and Mary found her mind wandering – drifting from scenario to scenario – accidental meetings with Terry – purposeful confrontations – any number of scripts. As her imagination began to run riot – the scenes she envisaged were more dramatic, more unlikely and far more entertaining than the simple story line of the very ordinary film being played out in front of her, on the television set.

NINETEEN

Far away, in Borneo, Tom's parents were arguing. Mrs. Livingstone was packed and ready to go to the airport. Her husband, as was his custom, was giving her instructions. Not for the first time she felt that he was talking to her like some underling in his office. She was becoming more and more angry and suddenly she had had enough.

"Right, that's it! Either you trust me to go to England and deal with this situation with Tom, or you don't!" She had got to her feet and her voice was strong. "If your work is more important than your son's health and welfare, so be it. I am more than happy to take responsibility for Tom but what I am not prepared to do is to go there as your lackey, your mouthpiece – your puppet in all this. You stay here and you forfeit your right to make the decisions. I shall be the one on the spot – I, not you, will speak to the professionals. I shall see Tom and speak to him and more importantly, listen to what he has to say. And then, I, and I alone, will decide what has to be done. Are you listening, Trevor. My decisions will be final. I will not have you bullying and badgering me on the telephone, nor will I have you coming over at Christmas and reversing any of my decisions!"

Trevor Livingstone was aghast. His wife had never, in all the time he had known her, spoken to him like that. He had to admire this new side to her character. He stammered over his words, "Well, yes.... Em..... I suppose you have a point. But...."

"No buts, Trevor. I am very serious about this. I want you to agree to bow out of this one. Do you understand?"

"Very well. As you like – but you will tell me what is happening – keep me informed?"

"Yes, I'll do exactly that – I will tell you what is happening –

what I have decided!" She emphasized every word.

The taxi had arrived. She picked up her hand luggage, kissed her husband on the cheek and, with her head held high, she left the room.

As soon as she reached the taxi her legs gave way and she allowed herself to crumble into the soft leather of the limousine. She felt as if she had been watching her own performance – "Bravo!" she said to herself, "Well done!"

She had wanted to do that for years. Her mother, she knew, would have been proud of her. She had been telling her to stand up to Trevor for a long time.

The knotted feeling in her solar plexus began to ease a little, for the first time, since she had heard of her young son's flight from school. She was going to make it right for him. She had been silent for too long. She had allowed his father to bully him and she had allowed herself to be manipulated into trying to toughen up her gentle little boy to suit his father's preconceived ideas. She had so many regrets, so much guilt but at least she now had a chance to try to put things right.

She hoped that the damage that had been done was not irreversible. Thank goodness she was on her own. It was a blessing that Trevor would not be joining them for several weeks yet. This gave her time to begin the healing with Tom. A macho father figure was the last thing her son needed at this time!

TWENTY

Mary gradually adjusted to being on her own again and indeed she needed this time. She had not realised how much all the emotional turmoil had drained her physically. When she left the safety of her house she felt vulnerable and was aware of her insecurity. She kept looking over her shoulder and jumping at shadows. She was very sure now that this could not be allowed to go on.

Her greatest test was approaching but it would lead her, through a gateway, to freedom. It was therefore, a confused mixture of anticipation and considerable fear which surrounded her, whenever she thought about what lay ahead.

Her home was no longer cut off from the outside world. Her telephone seemed to ring quite often considering how few people knew her number. Dr. Jacobs rang to give her an update on Tom. Tom rang her to ask about Shadow and Howard rang her to ask how she was coping. It all felt wonderful to Mary and she realised just how much she wanted this kind of normality and how much she had missed it.

Mary was sitting by the patio window gazing out over the garden. It had taken on its autumnal look – shutting down for the onset of winter. The grass had stopped growing – the herbaceous plants had almost finished flowering and the few remaining annuals which still bloomed seemed to sense that the first frost would soon herald their demise. Mary looked forward to the regrowth of the spring and the beginning of the new cycle once again. This next spring, she thought, would be a new beginning for her as well.

Perhaps she would make an offer for this house. She did love it and she felt so at home here now. Yes, perhaps she would buy it and build on a conservatory – modernise the bathroom. Her imagination had taken hold – she could buy a car and go on holiday. She could, she thought, do anything she wanted to do. She could take Tom on outings – to the zoo – to the donkey sanctuary. She sat smiling to herself – it was all there for the taking.

The telephone rang disturbing her daydreams. She got up slowly. It was Tom, "Hi, Mary, my Mummy's here. She wants to speak to you."

"Are you all right, Tom?" Mary asked feeling apprehensive.

"Yes. Everything is fine. Here's Mummy."

Tom's mother's voice sounded different – lower, gentler somehow than Mary remembered.

"Janey Livingstone, here. I wanted to thank you so much for taking such good care of Tom last week. I don't know what would have happened if you hadn't been there."

"I was only too glad to help. I care a lot for Tom."

"I know you do and I do appreciate all you did for him. I am taking what happened very seriously and am listening to the doctor's advice. Tom will not be returning to boarding school. We should never have sent him there. I let his father talk me into it but that is no excuse. I should have protected my son – put him first. Still, I am doing all that I can to put things right. I realise that Tom needs to keep a connection with his old home and his friends there and you seem to be top of his list and the cat, of course!"

"I would be only too happy to have Tom visit again, if you would allow it. Perhaps a weekend sometime. I hope to have a car before too long so I would be able to drive him back to you if you dropped him off here." Mary said.

"That would be fine – so perhaps in a few weeks, once he has settled in at his new school here, we could arrange it. I am staying on at my mother's until after Christmas."

The call finished with Tom having another word with Mary. He sounded happy and Mary felt a great load lift off her shoulders. She had to smile – getting a car before long – it had just come out so easily and she knew it was true.

Later that day the phone rang again. This time it was Howard.

"Can I come over? I have a report back on Terry. There's no need to worry about my car being seen at your door, is there?" he laughed ruefully. He still felt guilty about what had happened.

"Yes, any time. I've nothing planned. Why don't you come for dinner?"

"Right, I'll come straight from the office. Around six thirty?"

Mary put down the phone. Another first – a dinner guest! The changes seemed to be rushing in and she seemed able to cope. It was as if the walls which she had erected all around herself were falling down and it was she who was pulling them down.

She was not used to entertaining. It was such a long time since she had cooked for anyone other than herself. She had planned a pasta dish for herself so this was easily extended and, with a crisp green salad and some garlic bread from the freezer, it was easily prepared. She set the table in the kitchen with care and found a bottle of wine in the larder. She felt young again – 'again' seemed the wrong word to Mary. She could not, in all honesty, remember such a contented feeling from her youth. How long ago it all seemed!

When Howard arrived carrying a wrapped bottle shaped package as well as a manila folder he said, "Shall we eat first and then talk business? Don't let's spoil our meal with heavy conversation."

Mary agreed and they sat opposite one another talking like old friends. Mary told him the good news about Tom and how different his mother had seemed and what she had said about the car she was going to buy. "I can't tell you how surprised I was to hear myself announce its imminent arrival like that. It made me feel great. I sounded so positive and in control. It was wonderful."

Howard smiled as he tried to understand. He found it impossible to envisage how bad things had been for Mary. He knew that he had not the faintest idea of how terrible her life had been over all these years. However the fact that he acknowledged this inability gave Mary a feeling of acceptance and validation.

When they moved to the other room with their coffee Howard opened the beige folder, "This is the report so far from our private eye." He handed her the pages from inside the folder.

"I feel as if I am acting in some seedy scene from an old movie. It just doesn't seem real somehow." Mary said, putting off the moment when she would have to look at the material in front of her.

She eventually took a deep breath, reached for her reading glasses and looked down. It was all very neatly presented – done on a word processor – headings and dates and times underlined. It was easy to read.

Terry was still using his own name. He had apparently changed his car following the incident with the police outside her house. He was now driving a green transit van – the number was given. He lived in a bed and breakfast place about thirty miles away and he was working as an insurance salesman. He would be very good at that, Mary thought – especially selling to women. He had been in this area for a few months.

Mary swallowed as she read the next section of the report. It appeared that Terry had been spending a considerable amount of time doing some research into the history of the church opposite Mary's house. This apparently involved making a number of sketches in the graveyard area. Whenever the weather was suitable he would spend hours at a time there. He had also spoken at length with the vicar and the verger. He had also been asking questions of the owner and her assistant at the tea rooms next to the bank in the High street. He was not going away that was certain.

Mary had a feeling deep inside – it was not, as she might have expected, one of fear or even anger, it was, she decided, a feeling of irritation, a niggling feeling of a shoe rubbing on a blister, an unpleasant smell, a piece of grit in the eye. Something relatively minor but something which had to be dealt with. She was gazing into space.

"There are some photographs underneath." Howard interrupted her thoughts.

Mary moved the papers aside. There he was – how very ordinary he looked. This middle aged man in the pictures bore little resemblance to the handsome charmer she had remembered. He was, she supposed, good looking and she was sure that he still possessed the soft voice and the sugary words which went with it. She shivered slightly then. But no, when she looked at this man, she felt nothing – he was no threat to her – not any more and she knew that she could face him and tell him so. Now, because of this report, she was in control and she knew where she would be able to find him – across the road in the graveyard. What a fitting place to bury the past once and for all!

"Thank you, Howard. You were right. This is exactly what I needed. I can do it now. I'm ready to confront him and let him see the person I have become. It will all be over soon."

She looked so calm, so controlled. Howard was surprised. He had expected a different reaction. He had been dreading showing her these documents and especially the photographs.

"I'll come with you, if you like" he said.

"No, no, that wouldn't do at all. You must see that I have to do this alone. I have to do it by myself. It has to be this way. Just think, if it is a decent day tomorrow, it will all be over. I'll be free!"

They smiled at one another as they both lifted their coffee cups in a gesture of good luck.

Howard left soon after appreciating that Mary needed some time to reflect. "Ring me if you need me or want to talk," he said as he left, thanking her for the meal as he closed the door.

That night Mary felt fired up like the athlete who had trained religiously for four years ready for one Olympic bid. She was ready, primed and eager to get on with the task. The work had all been done. She was fully prepared. She did not need to make any plans. She had rehearsed and visualised this meeting with Terry so many times over the last months – she was certain that the next morning would be the time and the churchyard would be the place.

TWENTY ONE

Terry was feeling extremely frustrated. He seemed to be making little headway in reaching Rachel. He was as certain as he could be that Mary Parker was indeed his ex wife – as certain as he could be without seeing her with his own eyes. He had spent hours in the cold, in that god forsaken graveyard opposite her house, making rough sketches of tombstones and ancient architectural corners of supposed interest. There had been no activity at all in the area of the house with the blue door and Mary could be in hospital or on holiday, lying on some sun drenched beach. He could be freezing himself outside an empty house for all he knew.

He had spoken to the vicar a few times and managed to get him talking about the houses opposite and their occupants. He now knew that Mary Parker had been there a comparatively short time and that she was renting the house and that she lived alone. He also knew that she helped with the flowers in church and was a regular attender, usually at the early service, on Sunday mornings. Terry planned to be at that service on the following Sunday.

Terry had become a regular at the café in the High Street and had managed to ask about an old friend of his mother's who, he thought, lived somewhere close to the church. The two ladies who worked there then gave him a potted history of all the occupants in the houses in that area of town.

Mary Parker, he was told, was a bit odd – a bit of a recluse – kept herself to herself. Nobody knew much about her. No one knew if she had any family or where she had come from. It was apparent that this was a bone of contention to these two ladies who liked to know everyone's business. He did find out that the people who had lived next door to Mary had recently left – gone overseas for a

115

couple of years and the kiddies sent off to boarding school. Mary, they had heard, had been quite friendly with the little boy and had taken in a kitten for him when he wasn't allowed to keep it at home.

Terry had decided that he would give the churchyard one more day then leave it until the Sunday service in church. Perhaps, he thought, it would be best if he stayed in the van on Sunday morning and watched Rachel's door from there. He might be too conspicuous inside the church – especially at the early service. A stranger would attract a lot of attention in such a setting.

Luckily he had a van now and he had never parked it near the church so it would be safe enough to sit outside Rachel's house for a short time. He wanted no more confrontations with the police if he could help it.

Terry sat, perched on his canvas stool, beside an old gravestone. It stood at an angle and the inscription on the front was so worn that it was impossible to make out the name. He stared at the stone – occasionally letting his eyes move across towards the distant blue door.

"Thank, God!" he said to himself, "this is the last time I'll sit here like this." He hated the place and this town. Once he and Rachel were back together they would, he decided, move away – somewhere really up market. They would buy a beautiful house – one with a long driveway – room for several cars – maybe a swimming pool or a tennis court. Terry was enjoying himself – his imagination given free reign.

It wouldn't be like it was before. They would be happy, the two of them, with all that money. They could go on long exotic holidays – see the world. Yes, it was time to put the past behind them and start afresh. It was all going to work out just perfectly. He knew that Rachel needed him. She still wasn't well and she would need someone she could rely on. He had come along at the right time – before that smarmy, solicitor fellow, in his flashy sports car, got his feet under her table. It was obvious what he had in mind.

Terry was going over all of this in his head when suddenly the blue door opened. He couldn't believe it – Rachel was coming out at last. He saw a tall, slim woman step through the doorway. He knew it was her, even though she seemed to have changed so much. She was wearing a long skirt, wide and flowing, and neat black ankle boots with laces. She had on a thick, brightly coloured, woollen jacket with big pockets and her hair was pulled back out of sight, hidden underneath a black velvet hat. She was wearing tinted glasses and did not seem to be carrying a bag.

To his horror she was crossing the street and heading straight towards the church. She must be going in to see to the flowers, he thought, as he tried to pull himself in behind the crooked gravestone. She would have to walk almost past him. He bent his head down and concentrated on his notebook turning his head away from the direction of the church.

He could hear the sound of her boots on the paving stones. He was holding his breath waiting to hear the sound of the church door being unlocked..... The footsteps halted but there was no sound of the door opening......

"Hello, Terry." A low pleasant voice said, "I hear you have been looking for me!"

His mouth fell open and he jerked round, almost toppling off the tiny stool. He looked up into the beautiful, mature face of his ex wife. He felt awkward and rather stupid perched on his silly little stool.

This was a moment Mary would never forget. This was the culmination of all her work. She felt strong and confident and, for the first time in her life, in complete control. She had not hesitated for a single second. She felt as if she were a guided missile – steadily making its way towards its target. There could be no turning back – the outcome was preordained.

She felt as if she floated across the road – towards the church. As soon as she opened her front door she had seen the man on the stool in the churchyard and she knew that he had seen her. She was calm and composed and to her surprise, she realised, that she was enjoying herself. She smiled to herself as she saw Terry try to become invisible as she approached. He could not escape – there was nowhere to hide.

When Terry looked up at her from his crouched position she enjoyed his discomfiture. He struggled to his feet – dropping his pad and pencils as he did so.

"Rachel..." he stammered. "Is it really you?"

She looked at this man. Why, she wondered, had she ever worried about seeing him again. He was so ordinary – so pathetic – so second rate! He seemed smaller than she had remembered and he was certainly beginning to show his age. The age gap between them seemed greater than ever. The years had not been kind to him. She said nothing – just looked at him – her expression giving nothing away.

Terry was uncertain but was thinking on his feet as always.

"Oh, Rachel, it is so good to see you. You look so well. I heard about your father – I was so sorry....."

I just bet you were, Mary thought. She still did not speak.

"I can't believe you are standing there." Terry continued. "When I heard about your father, I tried to find you. I wanted to make sure that you were all right but you had disappeared. Nobody could tell me where you were."

"So you broke into a lawyer's office and managed to find out my new name. Then you tracked me down. Is that how it was, Terry?"

"Well, it wasn't quite like that....." He was struggling – floundering in the water like a drowning man. "None of that matters any more. I am just so glad to have found you!"

"And why is that, Terry?" She asked, an icy edge to her voice. She was watching him squirm.

"Don't be like this, Rachel. Let's forget the past. Let bygones be bygones, so to speak. What we once had was very special. I've never.."

"That's enough. Don't start...." She cut in.

"I'm sorry, Rachel." He was ready to grovel now and it sickened her. "I never meant for it to turn out the way it did. I made some mistakes, I know that. But I've changed."

"I'm pleased to hear that, Terry, but what has all this to do with me?"

"I would like a chance to make it up to you, if you'd let me." He was clutching at straws

"Yes, you can do something to make it up to me...."

"Anything, just say the word." Terry drooled, relaxing a little – this was better, he thought.

"Get the hell out of my life..." Rachel said, stressing each word, "and never come within a hundred miles of me again.......!"

When she spoke he saw for the first time that Rachel truly was her father's daughter. The vast fortune was not all that she had inherited from him. In that moment he knew that he had lost. This woman bore no resemblance to the young girl he had seduced and skillfully reduced to a quivering pawn in his game. He knew when he was beaten.

Without another word and leaving his things abandoned beside the gravestone he walked away without a backward glance.

Mary bent down and, with distaste, picked up the book and the pencils and the shabby canvas stool, dropping them carelessly into a rubbish bin.

It was done – she had done it. I was all over. She was free....!

TWENTY TWO

Mary let herself into the house and closed the door behind her. She felt most peculiar – neither exhilarated nor deflated – neither happy nor sad. She was surprised. She had expected to be either shouting from the rooftops or shaking like a leaf but she felt neither of these things. She felt calm and quiet and she sat down on a chair trying to analyse her emotions. Just then the telephone rang and she picked it up. It was Howard – he sounded anxious.

"Well I've done it!" She said, "I've sent him packing. It's all over!"

"Are you all right? Do you want me to come over?" Howard inquired, obviously unsettled by the lack of emotion in her voice.

"No, I'm fine – I really am. I think I want to be on my own today. I need a bit of time to digest all that's gone on. I'll come up to town tomorrow. Can you meet me for lunch then – my treat. Say, The Pompadour, at twelve thirty? I'll tell you all about it then."

Howard had no choice but to agree.

Mary went quietly into the kitchen and made a drink then returned to the couch and sat down, gazing through the window and beyond, seeing nothing – thinking nothing. She sipped her tea and stroked the cat who, at some time, had climbed onto her knee quite unnoticed.

It was quite some time before Mary came back from wherever she had been. When she returned she was full of energy. She went upstairs, had a shower and changed all her clothes. Everything she had had on she dropped into a black plastic bag and she put the bag into the dustbin. Then she opened the door into the garden and walked quickly through the garden and into the field. She had a great urge to run and run she did – faster and faster across the meadow until she collapsed in a breathless, hysterical heap beside the stream. She did not notice the dampness of the grass – she lay on her back and laughed!

"Get the hell out of my life!" she said it again and collapsed into even more laughter. Quite suddenly the laughter stopped and she said out loud, "Did I do O.K., Daddy?" and she knew that wherever he was, he was laughing too!

That was, for Mary, a peculiar day. She was not able to settle. She picked up her journal but words would not flow. She sat at her piano but her fingers would not dance. She stood by her easel but her creativity was asleep. She tried to meditate but her body fidgeted. She kept moving from room to room, from activity to activity. To her surprise, she ended up, in the kitchen baking a cake. She had never baked for years and she was amazed to find the ingredients she required in her cupboard. Of all things to do, on this day of all days.

She was sitting by the kitchen table admiring her achievement as it cooled on the wire rack. She smiled to herself as she realised that she had all the ingredients she needed to start her new life – all she had to do was reach for them and mix, blend and bake and something truly wonderful would be the result.

Just at that moment her door bell rang. She jumped in surprise and for a moment the old habit of fear clutched at her chest. She knew now that it would not be Terry. She knew for certain that he would never be back. She approached the door with a new freedom and for the first time opened it wide in a welcoming manner. She had nothing to hide and nothing to run away from. It felt marvellous.

Outside, on the doorstep, stood Tom's mother. She was obviously taken aback at the warmth of her welcome and looked round to see if some special friend had arrived behind her. She could not believe the change that had taken place in the woman who had been her neighbour for almost four years. She looked years younger, her eyes sparkled, her skin glowed and the haunted look and seriousness had gone from her face.

"Come in, Mrs. Livingstone. It's so nice to see you. How is Tom?" Even the voice had changed. Had Mary not called her by name she might have wondered if this woman was not in fact Mary's sister or some other close relative.

She was ushered through to the kitchen and offered tea and pressed to try a slice of home made cake.

Mary was not the only one who had changed. This woman, seated at her kitchen table was not the same person who had lived next door since Mary moved here. She seemed stronger, more self reliant and self assured – she was a much warmer, nicer person. Mary wondered if this was just her own changes reflecting back – a rosy glow falling on everything. But no, it was more than that.

Tom's mother, who she was now calling Janey, had come back to Ashtonbury to consult with Dr. Jacobs and had decided to call, in person, to thank Mary again for her kindness to her son.

There was a new closeness between the two women – drawn together by their mutual love for Tom and Mary decided, in that moment, to free herself of that last secret. She realised that to be with Tom, from now on, she had to be honest and open up to his mother about her past. It was, she felt, only fair to Dr. Jacobs and to Howard who had both taken such a risk by allowing Tom to stay here with her under such circumstances.

Once she began her story it was easy. She told it all. The lady opposite who, until a few minutes ago, had known little or nothing about her was now sharing in her innermost darkest secrets – her awful past.

Janey Livingstone sat quietly – fascinated and intrigued by Mary's story. Gradually as her story reached its climax and the final confrontation of that very morning, she understood. She did not recognise herself as she moved towards Mary and drew her into her arms and said, "Well done – Congratulations!"

The two women drew apart both with tears in their eyes and laughed.

"I thought you ought to know to whom you would be entrusting your son. It seemed only fair. But I do promise that I would never do anything to hurt him."

Janey answered quietly, "There is no one I would trust him with more," and she meant it. "You are a remarkable woman and I feel that you could teach me a great deal."

The two, who had become friends only that afternoon, sat down again and had another cup of tea.

The next day Mary dressed carefully for her lunch appointment. She was feeling energised and alive. There was a lightness in her step. She left her tinted glasses at home. As she made her way towards the bus stop she smiled and said good morning to everyone she met. She waved cheerily to the ladies in the tea room as she passed the door.

"What's gotten into her?" they commented to one another. "She's certainly not herself!"

Mary was first to arrive at the restaurant and she sat at the corner table and ordered a glass of white wine. Howard came hurrying in, apologising for being late. He was clutching some papers. "These are for you," he said smiling. She looked down and laughed. He had brought her brochures for cars and holidays.

You look terrific!" he said. "Come on, tell me all. I'm dying to hear all about it."

"So........" she finished as they sipped coffee from chunky brown cups, "I am free at last and it feels unbelievable. I want to tell everyone – hand out my address to all and sundry. Tell them who I am."

"And who are you – Mary or Rachel?" Howard asked, looking serious.

Mary stopped for a moment, thinking, "I think I am Mary Parker from now on but I am not ashamed, nor afraid, of who I used to be.

"I'm glad. You'll always be Mary to me – and who can tell about the Parker – maybe that will change one day......." He looked at her strangely.

"Who knows......." She smiled.

As Mary sat on the bus going home that afternoon she wondered about that look. Had she imagined it? 'Mary Hamilton! she mused. It did have a certain ring to it. She felt like a young girl again. She was starting all over and this time with a mature, confident head on her shoulders. Wasn't life just wonderful..........?

EPILOGUE

Terry Harrison had been travelling abroad for about three years. He had had enough of bumming around – conning his way around Europe – from one scam to another – one woman to another. He was tired and he was feeling old.

He was waiting for a connecting flight to Manchester and as usual he had latched on to an unescorted matron. They chatted amicably as they waited, Terry turning on the charm. He had used these techniques so long and so constantly that he knew no other way to behave.

The elegant lady excused herself and headed towards the ladies wash room. Terry sighed and picked up the copy of the Times which she had laid aside when he joined her. It was folded open at the Announcements and casually he ran his eye over the names. The name Hamilton caught his eye and he read on....

Howard and Mary Hamilton are delighted to announce the safe arrival of their two beautiful children – Rachel Harriet and Thomas Oldfield......

Terry gasped and read the names again. There could be no doubt. So Rachel had married the solicitor – he was not surprised. She had the children she always wanted......

As he placed the paper on the table in front of him he thought, 'I'm glad for her' – and he really meant it.